GIRLS
TO THE
RESCUE®
BOOK #6

*Tales of clever, courageous girls
from around the world*

EDITED BY BRUCE LANSKY

Meadowbrook Press

Distributed by Simon & Schuster
New York

Library of Congress Catalog Card Number: 95-17733

Publisher's ISBN: 0-88166-331-X
Simon & Schuster Ordering # 0-689-82574-9

Editor: Bruce Lansky
Coordinating Editor: Jason Sanford
Copyeditors: Jason Sanford and Christine Zuchora-Walske
Production Manager: Joe Gagne
Production Assistant: Danielle White
Cover Illustrator: Joy Allen

p. 1 "Dead Wrong" © 1999 by Carol Farley; p. 15 "Ginger Murphy Goes to Sea" © 1999 by Jon Picciuolo; p. 27 "Carmelina" © 1999 by Patricia Russo; p. 39 "Message in the Music" © 1999 by Carol Ottolenghi-Barga; p. 53, 99 "Lily and the Darters" and "Ang Pemba and the King's Riddle" © 1999 by Timothy Tocher; p. 61 "Samantha's Dog-Gone Adventure" © 1999 by Kelli Marlow Allison; p. 75 "Chita's Garden" © 1999 by Diane Sawyer; p. 85 "Shannon Holmes's First Case" © 1999 by Stephen Mooser.

Published by Meadowbrook Press, 5451 Smetana Drive, Minnetonka, Minnesota 55343

BOOK TRADE DISTRIBUTION by Simon & Schuster, a division of Simon and Schuster, Inc., 1230 Avenue of the Americas, New York, NY 10020

03 02 01 00 99   12 11 10 9 8 7 6 5 4 3 2 1

Printed in the United States of America

Dedication

This book is dedicated to my daughter, Dana. I used to make up stories for her when she was young, hoping to inspire her to believe in herself and to pursue her dreams. It is in that spirit that I have written and collected the stories in this series.

Acknowledgments

Thank you to all the young women who served
on a reading panel for this project:

Hayley Anderson, Jessica Austin, Erica Bezotte, Kristen Breault, Jackie Brown, Samantha Byrne-Bitzan, Sarah Byrne-Bitzan, Olivia Carlyle, Emma Cartwright, Ruthie Christianson, Catherine Colwell, Demi Lee Cooper, Kathy Cosmano, Katie Culhane, Courtney Darnell, Joanna Desautels, Morgan Dewanz, Cinthya Diaz, Natalie Dimberg, Jenny Dvorak, Brooke Ellison, Breanna Ellsworth, Liz Ennis, Krystan Nicole Fields, Jenny Ford, Sara Ford, Suzy Foster, Megan Frank, Marisa Fredrickson, Breanna Game, Jessica Gethardt, Heather Gilbertson, Emily Goplen, Beth Gucinski, Janelle Hamre, Jessica Hendrix, Tara Hengeler, Amanda Holmer, Amanda Impola, Alyssa Jacobs, Andrea Johnson, Melissa Johnson, Kasey Jones, Marie Jubert, Alynn Kakuk, Nicole Knapek, Jessica Kempe, Kristin Kordovsky, Anna Kornahrens, Christie Kostreba, Becca Krauss, Sarah Larson, Randi Launderville, Crystal Law, Kalyca Lawrence, Noel Lehmkuhl, Rebecca Lindquist, Megan Magdzas, Paige Maki, Stephanie Malmgren, Elyse Michaelsen, Alexandra Moeller, Ellen Moleski, Nicole Moleski, Emily M'mma, Anna Myhre, Michelle Neary, Ashley Nelson, Jessica Osceola, Danielle Peterson, Melissa N. Pleiss, Elizabeth Poole, Melissa Roers, Sarah Rolson, Carrie Rutten, Kristina Salas, Zoe Setright, Lina Sieverling, Elisabeth Smeltzer, Krista Sorensen, Mindy Spring, Kascie Sturtevant, Leah Thielmann, Rachael Turner, JoAnn Tyrdik, Laurie Verant, Vanessa Wagner, Kimberly Waldorf, Abby Warmboe, Caitlin Webb, Kristen Wood

Contents

Introduction

Do you like stories about danger and excitement? Or maybe you love to read stories about heroines who use their brains to triumph over adversity? In either case, *Girls to the Rescue, Book #6,* is the book for you. Here is a preview of some of the most exciting stories:

• Ginger Murphy, the daughter of a Coast Guard mechanic, knows almost as much about boat engines as her father—even though she's scared of the sea. Nonetheless, she agrees to replace her sick father in the engine room of a rescue boat during a violent storm to save some shipwrecked sailors from a sinking freighter.

• Gianna is a twelve-year-old living in occupied Italy during World War II. Her sick baby sister needs medical attention, so Gianna braves the dangers of the German patrols in order to find a doctor.

• Sally is a young slave who discovers that her brother is to be sold. She risks her life (and his) in a daring escape to freedom.

• Ang Pemba, who lives in the shadows of the Himalaya Mountains, has always wanted to be a royal sherpa—a mountain guide. To be chosen, she disguises herself as a boy. When disaster strikes and one of the other candidates for the job slips off a thin bridge, Ang Pemba risks her life to save him—even though her actions may uncover her true identity.

I think you'll agree that all of these stories contain plenty of excitement. However, I believe you'll also be intrigued by other stories in this book—stories that are more about brains than brawn:

• Samantha's keen powers of observation and deductive reasoning enable her to solve a mystery when dogs and cats in her neighborhood begin to disappear.

• Shannon Holmes, Sherlock Holmes's clever niece, does a fine bit of detective work to solve two mysteries at a horse race.

• To prove her intelligence and gain entry into a boys-only school, Lily, a clever Chinese girl, captures a dragonfly— something none of the boys can do.

As you can see, the new heroines in *Girls to the Rescue, Book #6*, are worthy additions to those you have already met (or should meet!) in the first five books in the series. In short, I'm happy to say that we've served up another entertaining collection of stories about smart, spunky girls who save the day.

Bruce Lansky

Dead Wrong

AN ORIGINAL STORY BY CAROL FARLEY

Lumberjack Jargon:
Flaggins: bread and tea served in a bucket.
Choppers: lumberjacks who cut down trees.
Sawyers: lumberjacks who saw cut-down trees into logs.

Candlelight flickered across the page. Kristen bent over her letter, biting her lip as she guided the quill across the paper, taking care not to drip any ink. Writing to Edith wasn't nearly as much fun as talking to her. Kristen recalled the many hours she'd spent talking, laughing, and playing with her best friend.

Then she sighed, stretched her cramped hand, and kept writing:

November 1, 1848

Dear Edie,

Do you miss me? I miss you, but I'm really excited about being here. Even after four days I can hardly believe I'm truly living in a lumber camp in Manitoba. Not many girls get to do that! I'll write as often as I can to tell what's happening. I can send and receive letters through Brody's Store, so be sure to write me, too.

I'm so glad Pa finally agreed that I'm old enough to help him in the cook shanty this winter. I miss you and Aunt Anna, but I want to be with him.

I love being in the forest. The pine trees are enormous! When I go walking among them, I feel like I'm in church. Isn't that the strangest thing?

There's somebody else here about my age. Nels Johansen was the chore boy for the cook before Pa. Now he's a sawyer. That's what they call the men who saw the trees into logs once the choppers have cut them down. See how much I've learned about lumber camp already?

You'll never guess what I saw my first day here. Two of the most beautiful white swans! I was down by the river when—

"You got anything good to eat in here, Kristen?"

Kristen looked up from her letter and cupped her hand around the candle to protect it from the cold gusts that entered the cook shanty with Nels Johansen. Nels slammed the door and stomped snow off his big boots. The snowflakes dotting his hat and jacket were more numerous than the freckles dotting his red face. Nels flushed even redder when he glanced around and saw that Kristen was alone.

"We've got lots to eat," Kristen said, rising quickly and covering the ink pot. "I just took bread out of the oven. Pa's out getting more logs right now."

"Guess that cold wind made me hungrier than usual," Nels murmured as he moved toward the stove. "It's snowing hard, too. Winter's coming mighty fast."

As if to confirm Nels's words, a fierce wind rattled the wooden shack. Kristen glanced out the window. It wasn't yet five o'clock, and night was already falling. She knew winter always arrived early in the heart of Canada. She also knew that Nels was more interested in talking than eating, so she stood quietly beside him after handing him a slice of bread. Nels was too shy to talk to anyone else in camp, Pa had told her, but from the very first day he had talked eagerly to Pa and her.

He took a bite, then glanced her way. "Do you know Mr. Bergman?"

Kristen was slowly getting to know all the men in the camp—and the wife of the camp foreman, too. But Mr. Bergman spent most of his time with his oxen, so she barely saw him. "I've seen him," she said.

Nels looked down at the stove. "He was talking in the bunkhouse this morning. He says a cook's chore boy ought to be a boy."

"Well!" Kristen straightened her shoulders. "I can do every single thing a boy could do to help Pa cook!"

"That's true; that's true," Nels quickly agreed, sorry he had upset her. "Maybe all teamsters are contrary. Maybe mean, too. The one we had before Mr. Bergman came two weeks ago used to whip Effie and Junie until they bled!"

"That's terrible, Nels! Does Mr. Bergman do that, too?"

"Don't know. We're not working near him right now. I think that other fellow loaded the wagons too full. Effie and Junie struggled to pull their loads, but—"

Once again the door flew open. Pa staggered in, his arms full. Kristen wanted to hear more about Mr. Bergman and the oxen, but after helping Pa stack the logs, Nels hurried back outside.

All evening, Kristen kept busy helping Pa make dinner for the camp. She'd have to finish her letter another day.

The next day, Kristen thought about what Nels had said as she took lunch to the men. The men in the woods were happy to see her. They smiled and shouted their thanks for the bread and tea they called "flaggins."

But Mr. Bergman, down by the river with Effie and Junie, barely nodded when he saw her. She quickly handed him his flaggins, then hurried off to the backwater where the river had been diverted. This huge, deep pond would hold the logs before they were sent downriver in the spring. It held no logs yet. But it did hold something else—something magical.

Eagerly Kristen searched the freezing water. Yes! The two beautiful white swans were still there, gliding across the water as gracefully as ballet dancers across a stage. She reached for the bread in her pockets, just as she had done for four days now. The swans saw her and swam her way. For a long time she stood there, hidden in the brush, feeding the swans and feeling happy as she breathed the frosty air.

Crack! A harsh noise shattered the quiet. Kristen

ran to the riverbank just in time to see Mr. Bergman raise his whip again. It flew over the loaded wagon and the oxen's backs like a vicious black snake. Crack! Angrily she whirled around and raced back to the cook shanty.

"Pa, I saw Mr. Bergman whipping the oxen!" Kristen cried as the door slammed behind her. "You've got to tell him to stop! He loads the wagon too heavy for Effie and Junie."

"Now, now, my girl." Pa set down the huge soup kettle he'd been carrying. "We've got no right to tell others how to do their jobs."

"But he's hurting them!"

"Are you sure about that? Oxen are tough beasts. Bergman knows the whole camp depends on Effie and Junie. He wouldn't do anything to cause real harm. Besides, soon's we get more snow, he'll be using the sled. That's a lot easier on the beasts."

"But will you talk to him? Until he can use a sled, will you ask Mr. Bergman not to whip Effie and Junie?"

"Nothing to talk about," Pa answered. For a few seconds Kristen stood quiet, sure that he was angry. But his next words were gentle. "Did you see those swans today?"

She nodded. "They were in the backwater again, close to where Mr. Bergman works. But I don't think he even notices."

"Maybe not. I'd guess that Bergman's like most lumberjacks. These men have spent their whole lives laboring in lumber camps. They've never been taught to appreciate the finer things in life." He shook his head. "Those swans ought to be heading south soon. If a hard freeze sets in quick-like, they could be in trouble way up north here."

"Like Effie and Junie," Kristen thought.

"I tried to help you," she whispered as she entered their dark stable several hours later. The oxen were standing at their trough, their faces buried in oats. Steam rose from their bodies and the pleasant odor of fresh hay filled Kristen's nose. She ran her hand across Effie's back and felt great welts. She gasped, sure that Mr. Bergman's whip was the culprit.

"What're you doing in here?" Mr. Bergman's voice boomed through the darkness. His beard bristled in the flickering lantern light and his breath hung like fog in the frigid air.

Kristen lowered her lantern. "I was just—"

"You stay away from my oxen!" he shouted as she

ran for the door.

The temperature plummeted that night. Kristen huddled cozily by the cookstove. Pa would rise at 3:30 to begin fixing breakfast, but she could sleep until 5:00. Then the whole camp would rise, eat, and be off for another day in the pine forest.

After breakfast, the cook shanty was toasty-warm as Kristen cleaned up. She hummed as she nibbled on leftover hot cakes and dried the dishes. Lunch time came quickly.

"Take Bergman's flaggins first," Pa said as he packed all the tin buckets. "He'll be down by the river, like yesterday. The other fellows are in the northern section. They'll be as hungry as horses in this cold weather."

Kristen bit her lip before she could blurt out the wrong words. If she had her way, Mr. Bergman could stay hungry.

When she stepped outside, the wind nearly took her breath away—and so did the dazzling landscape. The sun glistening on the snow made the ground look as though it were covered with diamonds. "I'll have to tell Edie about that," she decided as she walked. Then a more troubling thought crossed her mind. "If Mr. Bergman is whipping those oxen today, why, I'll . . ."

Her thoughts were jared by a spine-chilling bellow. The oxen! She dropped Mr. Bergman's bucket and raced toward the sound. Rounding the bend she saw the two oxen standing by the backwater, their wagon empty. Mr. Bergman was nowhere in sight.

Then she heard his voice. "Help!"

Stunned, she stared at the pond. Overnight the water had frozen. The surface lay pure and white, unmarked except by footprints leading to the middle. And there Kristen saw a terrifying sight. Mr. Bergman's head and arms stretched out from the icy-cold water. He had fallen through the ice and now, as he tried to climb out, chunks were breaking off as quickly as he grabbed for them.

"I'm coming!" Kristen screamed. She stepped onto the ice.

"Don't!" Mr. Bergman cried. "You'll fall through! Get the rope! By the wagon!"

Kristen bounded to the wagon, where Junie and Effie waited silently. She grabbed the mound of coils. How could she throw this? She needed to tie one end of the rope to something heavy. She looked around frantically and saw a huge hammer. Quickly, she knotted the rope to its head and ran back to the edge of the frozen pond. She tied the other end of the rope around her body and flung the hammer across the ice.

Mr. Bergman grabbed it. "Pull!" he screamed.

Kristen grabbed the rope with both hands and leaned back, pulling with all her weight. But nothing happened. Mr. Bergman was a big man, and with his waterlogged boots and clothes, he was too heavy for her to move.

"Pull harder!" he called, his voice weakening.

Desperately Kristen tried to think of a way to get more power. Her darting eyes fell on Junie and Effie. "Oh, you've got to help!" she moaned as she yanked the rope from her body and tied it to their harness. "Move!" she shouted, slapping Junie's flank. "Move, Junie, move Effie!"

But the oxen just stood there.

"They won't move!" she screamed to Mr. Bergman. His answer was too weak for her to make out. Kristen knew he could die soon from the frigid water. She had to do something fast. She turned to slap Junie again and stumbled over something lying on the ground. The whip! Did she dare use it? Mr. Bergman was sinking beneath the icy water. She had no choice.

Kristen seized the whip and cracked it high in the air.

The oxen jerked up their heads and instantly bolted forward. In moments they dragged Mr. Bergman to shore.

Less than an hour later, Mr. Bergman was sitting wrapped in a blanket in front of the cookstove. "I'm mighty grateful to you, Larson," he told Pa. He gestured at the stove. "You got me warmed up just in time." He looked at Kristen. "And I'm mighty grateful to you, too, miss. Grateful that you knew how to get Junie and Effie to help."

Kristen's throat tightened. "I hated using that whip."

"She thinks the whip hurts the oxen," Pa explained.

Mr. Bergman shook his head. "Depends on who's using it. Me, I get my beasts to do my bidding without letting the whip even touch them. The noise alone does the job. But the fellow before me here, why, he wasn't so gentle. Poor Effie and Junie still bear the scars, and I'm mighty sorry about that."

So that was why they had those welts on their backs. Kristen felt her face flush. She'd been wrong to blame Mr. Bergman for something he didn't do.

Pa leaned closer. "One thing I can't figure, Bergman. Why in tarnation were you walking on that ice?"

Mr. Bergman sat staring at the floor. Finally he raised his head. "Well, I'll tell you, but if you ever breathe a word of this, I'll deny it. You know them two swans? Well, I've been watching them in the backwater for a week now, and a prettier sight I've never seen. I kept wondering why they weren't heading south. The weather's getting mighty cold and no one's been feeding them to keep them here."

Kristen caught her breath. She'd been feeding them for days! Was that wrong?

"Anyway," Mr. Bergman went on, "when I went down to work this morning, they were still out in the middle of the pond, and they were making all kinds of racket. I didn't think much about it, just set to work.

"When it was time for lunch, I took a better look and saw that those birds had waited too long before flying south. They'd been sleeping with their feet dangling in the water, and the pond had frozen over, trapping them. They could no more get out of that mess than they could fly to the moon."

"It was my fault!" Kristen thought. She turned a stricken face toward Pa and saw that he realized she had been feeding the swans.

"So you went out to free them?" Pa asked Mr. Bergman.

"Sure did. They nearly pecked me to death before

they saw I was trying to help. I had them chopped out in no time. They were mighty happy to take off for the south, I'm sure. I must've stepped on some thin ice when I was heading for shore, because suddenly I was trapped. Couldn't get out of that mess to save my soul. Thank God your girl came along! Why, your Kristen here saved my life!"

Mr. Bergman looked at the floor. "I got to confess it. When I first heard that a girl was our cook's chore boy, I wasn't too happy. Didn't think a girl would be strong enough or smart enough to manage life in a lumber camp. But I was wrong. Dead wrong." He paused, then chuckled at his choice of words. "Or I guess I should say I was wrong but not dead, thanks to Kristen."

"I was wrong, too," Kristen mumbled.

"About what?" Mr. Bergman asked.

"About how many potatoes she needs to peel for tonight's supper," Pa put in quickly. He grinned in her direction. "Get a big kettle full, Kris. Tonight's fiddle night, you know, and the boys'll need lots of energy for singing."

Smiling, Kristen hurried to the potato bin. She'd been wrong to feed the swans. She'd been wrong about Mr. Bergman's treatment of animals. But he'd been wrong about something, too. Now he knew—and soon the whole camp would know—that a girl could do just fine in a lumber camp. She could hardly wait to tell Nels and write Edie all about it!

Ginger Murphy Goes to Sea

AN ORIGINAL STORY BY JON PICCIUOLO

The last hill on the road home was Ginger Murphy's favorite. As she trotted her pony over its crest, the wide Pacific Ocean spread out before her. The coast guard lifeboat rescue station where she lived was perched a mile ahead on a rocky cliff. She rode her pony hard and in a few minutes she was home. She led her frisky pony into the corral, fed him some hay, then ran into the kitchen of her cottage.

"Hi, Ma!" Ginger said, dropping her school books on a chair. "I'm hungry. What's for dinner?"

Her mother was shelling peas. "Fish."

Ginger made a sour face—she hated fish. But her mother didn't notice and continued talking.

"We'll be eating late tonight—there's a drill."

"A lifeboat drill? Can I watch?"

"Yes, but don't get in the way."

As Ginger pushed open the screen door, she shivered a little. Watching lifeboat drills could be fun. But she'd never, ever ride to sea in that little boat! The ocean frightened her—especially those towering, crashing waves.

The boys in the schoolhouse teased her sometimes. They wanted to know why the twelve-year old daughter of a coastguardsman feared the sea. In reply, she always asked why the sons of ranchers were afraid of bulls. Then—for a little while—they understood her.

When Ginger was halfway down the wooden stairs to the boathouse, she heard the coxswain shouting orders: "Start the engine! Engage the winch!" His next words were lost in the rumble of the lifeboat motor. The girl stood tall with pride—her father kept that old cranky engine repaired. He was in the boat now, operating the controls.

Ginger ran along the dock to where she could see the boathouse doors swing open. From the shadows emerged the white lifeboat. As it slid down the ramp, she could see the spinning bronze propeller.

The boat splashed into the water. With the engine growling, it circled the cove twice then headed to sea. If this were a real rescue, she knew, the lifeboat would speed to the shipwreck. However, this was just a drill and soon the boat returned to the dock.

"Hi, Ginger! Wanna go for a ride?" called the coxswain, spinning his wheel. Her father poked his head out of the cabin and waved at her.

"No, thank you," she answered politely.

Ginger watched as the boat was winched up the ramp. Its powerful engine was silent now. Gallons of seawater sloshed off the deck. "The waves must have been as high as mountains out there," she thought.

Her father was standing on the lifeboat's deck when she walked into the boathouse. "Come aboard, honey. Climb the ladder."

Ginger scrambled up and hugged her father.

"Do you want to see your favorite motor?" he asked with a wink.

She ducked into the boat's cabin. All the way in the back was a narrow hatch. The girl opened it and stepped into the tiny engine compartment. Light coming through two small portholes let her see.

"Hey, you replaced the cooling pump!" she said, pointing. "And that looks like a new oil line!"

Her father chuckled. "Tomorrow's Saturday—I'm changing the old guy's fuel filter and you can help. But there's something we have to do right now. The engine ran awful rough out there. Go up on deck and see if something's blocking the air intake."

"Can I help test the engine tomorrow?"

"Sure. What's mother fixing for dinner tonight?"

"Fish," Ginger said as she ducked through the hatch. "If I eat double vegetables, can I skip the fish?"

"Maybe," her father replied.

On deck Ginger walked quickly to the air intake, one of several small pipes near the stern. The intake's cover was missing, but that did not surprise her—seawater often rusted away small parts. She pulled a long strand of brown kelp from the pipe.

When she showed the seaweed to her father, he said, "Good girl! You found the problem. I'll replace that cover tomorrow."

That night Ginger's father ate his portion of fish and hers, too, while she contented herself with extra vegetables. After dinner her family listened to the radio. Soon she could hardly keep her eyes open; she kissed her parents and went to bed.

It was dark and very late when someone roughly shook her shoulder. She could hear men outside the cottage shouting about a shipwreck. The wind howled; rain splattered against the windowpanes.

"Wake up, Ginger," her mother said. "Your father's sick. The night train took him to the hospital. It must have been that fish."

"The fish? How do you feel, Ma?"

"Just a little queasy—I only had a small piece." Her mother's voice sounded weak. "Get up. The station commander wants to see us."

Ginger was wide awake now. "Chief Watkins? Why?"

"He'll tell you. Get dressed!"

The station commander's office was brightly lit. Chief Watkins was standing behind his desk, red-faced and shouting into the telephone.

"Hello, Arguello Lighthouse?" he bellowed. "Can you hear me? My engineman's in the hospital with food poisoning. Do you have anyone there who can operate a boat engine?" He listened to the reply, then shook his head. "No, Santa Barbara's too far—there's not enough time. Thanks anyway. Good-bye!" The chief slammed down the phone and waved Ginger and her mother into two chairs. His mustache quivered and bounced as he leaned across the desk.

"I heard you can run that boat engine, girl. Is this true?"

Ginger thought of the towering, plunging waves. She shuddered and gulped, then slowly said, "Well . . . maybe. But—"

Chief Watkins didn't let her finish. He turned to Ginger's mother and waved his hands. "A coastal freighter hit a rock and is sinking! Your girl's the only one who can keep that old rattletrap engine running. Will you give permission?"

Mrs. Murphy had only one question. "What happens if she doesn't go?"

The station commander slumped into his chair. "The men on that ship will drown."

"Then she'll go, Chief." Ginger's mother squeezed her daughter's hand.

"But, Ma, I'm scared—," Ginger began. Then she saw the awful look in Chief Watkins's eyes. "I'm scared . . . that I'm not good enough!"

"Nonsense!" shouted the chief. "Your father's the best and he taught you. You can do it! Now get going."

Her mother led Ginger to the top of the boathouse stairs. She hugged her daughter in the rain, then softly whispered, "I know you're frightened. Think of your father—do it for him."

Inside the boathouse, sweating coastguardsmen were loading the lifeboat with stacks of blankets, coils of rope, and jugs of hot coffee. Some of the men looked worried—they whispered and pointed at her.

The coxswain ordered them back to work. Then he announced loudly, so everyone could hear, "You're my engineman, Ginger. We're leaving in five minutes. Any questions?"

"Is it . . . is it rough out there?" she stammered.

"I've seen worse," he softly said with a smile. "You'll do fine. Obey my orders and remember what your father taught you. Now get aboard."

She climbed the ladder and made her way through the cabin and into the engine compartment. Recalling her father's warning about keeping the boat watertight, she shut the hatch firmly. The familiar smell of metal polish and diesel oil comforted her. She opened the main fuel valve and waited.

Suddenly, through a brass tube that came down from the boat's cockpit, she heard the coxswain's voice. "Start the engine!"

Ginger mashed the start button and whispered a little prayer. The wheezy engine stuttered a few times, then rumbled into action. The lifeboat tipped sharply as it slid down the ramp. There was a lurch and a splash. The boat rolled sickenly from side to side.

Suddenly the coxswain shouted a string of engine orders through the brass tube: "Reverse! Half speed ahead! Full speed ahead!" Forgetting her fear, Ginger tugged the control levers to and fro. She studied the oil pressure gauge carefully—when the needle dropped a bit, she surged the engine and kicked the oil pump. That leveled out the pressure like it always did.

As the boat roared through the cove, Ginger glimpsed the sea—and those giant waves—through one of the little glass portholes. She began to shiver.

The lifeboat slammed into the waves and boomed like a drum. Ginger braced herself against the engine and held on. Through the tiny portholes she watched foamy water swirl every time the wild sea swept across the deck. Many minutes passed.

Suddenly the engine's steady roar faltered. The coxswain shouted, "We're losing speed! What's wrong?"

"The engine's running rough," Ginger answered.

She remembered the missing cover. "I think something's stuck in the air intake. Can you clear it?"

The brass tube was silent for a moment, then the coxswain said, "My men can't find the intake. If that engine stops I'll lose control of the boat and we'll capsize! Come up here and fix the problem!"

Hot tears rolled down Ginger's cheeks. The engine sputtered twice and slowed. Her hands shook as she listened to the coxswain's next words.

"Leave the engine running! Put on a lifejacket and get up here right now! That's an order!"

She whispered a prayer and opened the hatch. Two pale coastguardsmen crouching on the benches helped her into an orange lifejacket. She climbed the steep stairs to the boat's cockpit. Salty spray soaked her face as she stared at the dark heaving sea.

"Here," said the coxswain, handing her a thick leather belt.

"Wh. . .why?" stammered Ginger as she pulled the belt tight.

"Everyone on deck wears a safety rope."

"On deck? But those waves—"

"Clear that intake and get back here as fast as you can!" He spun the wheel as the engine coughed and chugged, then he added in a low voice, "There's not much time, Ginger."

Shivering, she climbed down a steel ladder and staggered along the wooden deck to the stern. Just as she had feared, a wet handful of kelp was lodged deep in the air intake. As she pulled out the seaweed, the engine roared with new power. The lifeboat surged forward. Ginger lost her balance and tumbled into the icy water.

Seconds later, coughing and gasping, she was tugged back aboard.

"Thank God for that safety rope!" the coxswain yelled. "Just keep that engine running! Look, we're almost to the shipwreck." He pointed into the darkness. A distress rocket spit long red sparks as it climbed into the low clouds. In the rocket's red glow, Ginger could see a ship leaning hard to starboard, sinking fast.

Back in the engine room, the big motor thundered. Ginger twisted valves and adjusted controls. Just as she was wondering how much longer until they reached the ship, the coxswain shouted, "Reverse! Ahead slow! Stop the engine!"

There were bumps and scuffles on the deck above her head. Through the cabin's closed hatch, she heard muffled, confused voices. A man cried out in pain. When icy sea water sloshed over Ginger's shoes, she switched on the bilge pump. Ginger felt very alone. She found a torn rag and wiped down the engine for luck, just like her father did.

At last the coxswain yelled, "Start the engine! Full speed ahead, Ginger! We're going home!"

The heavy lifeboat wallowed and creaked. The old motor coughed and strained and began to overheat. Ginger opened a tiny valve on the cooling manifold; air hissed loudly, water spluttered out. The engine ran smoother. Sweat dripped down her cheeks. She rubbed off the wetness and glanced at her hand—it was filthy with grease.

"You're a real mess," she told herself.

When the coxswain ordered "Reverse," then "Ahead slow," Ginger realized the dock had to be very close. There was a sharp thump, followed by an order to stop the engine. A tired voice in the brass tube said, "We're home, Ginger. Come up on deck."

She opened the hatch and peered into the cabin. There, seated on the narrow benches, were a dozen miserable oil-soaked strangers staring back at her.

One of them pointed in open-mouthed surprise.

"Why, you're just a girl! A little kid! Who was really running that engine?"

Just as those stinging words were spoken, the station commander came into the cabin. "That young girl saved your lives," Chief Watkins said with a scowl. "You don't have to like it, but it's the truth!"

The stranger was silent for a moment, then murmured a word of thanks and offered his hand. Ginger shook it firmly. She stood out of the way as the shipwrecked men filed out of the cabin.

Chief Watkins put his big fists on his hips. "Your dad's going to be fine—the hospital says he just needs a little rest. So, girl, what do you think about waves now?"

"How . . . how did you find out about that?"

"Your mom told me. Are you still afraid of the sea?"

Ginger thought for a moment before she replied. "Well, the waves don't scare me anymore. But I sure haven't changed my mind about fish!"

Carmelina

AN ORIGINAL STORY BY PATRICIA RUSSO

Italian Words:

Beretto da notte (pronounced "be-RE-to da NO-te"): a frilly nightcap worn by women.

Farina (pronounced "fa-REE-na"): a cream-of-wheat-style cereal.

Cara: means "dear."

Carmelina lay motionless in Mama and Papa's big bed. A few hours ago, she'd been fussing and crying, trying to throw the covers off. Now she lay deathly still, her face waxy and white. "She looks like a wax statue," Gianna thought.

Mama touched Carmelina's forehead and whispered, "She's as hot as an oven."

"Is Carmelina going to be all right?" Gianna asked.

"I don't know."

"She has to be all right," Gianna said. Carmelina had been born in the middle of the war. She was only two; she couldn't die now that peace was so close.

"I don't know what to do," Mama said. Her voice was tight and shrill. Gianna could tell she was fighting back tears.

"We have to get the doctor."

"The doctor won't come, Gianna," Mama said.

"He has to come," Gianna insisted. "Carmelina's sick!"

"It's too dangerous," Mama said.

It was 1944. Italy had surrendered to the Allies a year ago. Immediately the German army had occupied much of the country. Italy and Germany had been on the same side; now they were enemies.

A squad of German soldiers had swept through the town of Garzano just a few days ago, looking for men: young, old, middle-aged—it didn't matter. Some were held hostage. Some were forced to join the German army. Some were simply shot.

Gianna's papa and her uncle Luigi had been hiding in the woods for almost a week. Most of the other men who lived in Garzano were hiding, too. Some were in an old barn a few miles outside of town. Some were in the school. Some were even hiding in the cemetery. Many, though, just stayed indoors and hoped the German soldiers wouldn't search their houses.

Gianna stroked her sister's cheek. Carmelina was burning up. She'd fallen sick two days ago and just kept getting worse.

"I'll fetch Dr. Fornaro," Gianna said. "He should be home. He's too old to hide in the woods. When I tell him how sick Carmelina is, I know he'll help."

Her mother frowned with fear. "No, Gianna. It's not safe."

"I'll take Papa's bicycle. I'll be quick."

"But the soldiers . . ."

"I'll be careful," Gianna said. "If I see any soldiers, I'll pedal away as fast as I can."

Mama gazed at her. Gianna knew what Mama was thinking: No matter how fast Gianna pedaled, she couldn't outpedal a bullet.

Gianna turned toward her little sister. Carmelina was breathing so shallowly the blanket barely moved. "I'm going," Gianna said. "I'll be back as soon as I can."

Mama bit her lip and nodded.

Papa's bicycle was heavy. Gianna wrestled it down the steps, panting. The seat was too high for Gianna, so she stood on the pedals. Pumping furiously, she tore down the street.

Garzano was silent. All the stores were closed, and the street was deserted. Gianna saw an old woman peeking from behind a curtained window. It was Signora Tozzato, her friend Maria's grandmother. The old woman must have just woken up. She was wearing a robe and a *beretto da notte*, a frilly cap that some old women wore to bed.

Gianna waved at her as she pedaled by. Signora Tozzato was keeping watch. Maria's house had a cellar, and her father and older brother were hiding there.

If Gianna looked over the roofs of Garzano, she could see a mountain in the distance. At the summit was an abbey called Monte Cassino. Benedictine monks had lived there for hundreds of years. Then the German army had taken it over.

Night after night, Allied planes bombed Monte Cassino. The bombs sounded like thunder. The sky lit up like a fireworks show. Carmelina was so scared of the bombs she would cry whenever a plane flew overhead. Then Papa would take her on his lap and say, "Don't be afraid. Those are American planes. They're our friends. They won't hurt you."

Gianna wished Papa was home. She knew Mama wouldn't be so scared then.

Dr. Fornaro lived in a small white house at the top of Via Pascoli, Garzano's main street. Gianna hopped off the bicycle and leaned it against the inside of Dr. Fornaro's garden wall. She dashed up the path.

Gianna knocked softly on the door so Dr. Fornaro would know she wasn't a soldier. When the soldiers came to search a house, they beat on the door with their fists. If nobody answered, they kicked the door down.

A curtain twitched in the window. After a long moment, the door opened a crack. "What is it?" the doctor whispered.

"My sister, Carmelina, is very sick," Gianna said softly. "Mama is afraid she's going to die."

The door opened a little wider. Dr. Fornaro stuck his head out and peered up and down the street. He was an old man with stooped shoulders and sparse white hair. But that wouldn't stop the German soldiers from arresting him. "Did you see anybody?" he whispered.

"No Germans saw me. Please, it's an emergency. Carmelina's fever is very high. Mama doesn't know what to do."

Dr. Fornaro sighed. "I know your house. Go on. Tell your mother I'll be there in a few minutes."

Gianna grinned. A wave of relief washed over her. "I knew you were a brave man, Dr. Fornaro," she said.

"Brave?" he said. "I've never been so frightened in my life. Now hurry. Your mother will be worried."

Gianna pedaled home furiously, hauled Papa's bike up the steps, and stowed it in the closet.

"Mama?" She ran upstairs to her parents' room. Mama sat on the bed, holding Carmelina's hand. "How is she?"

"I can't wake her up," Mama said, wiping away tears. "She's even hotter now than she was when you left."

"I talked to the doctor," Gianna said. "He'll be here soon."

Mama looked up and her tight face suddenly relaxed a little. "Thank God," she murmured.

Fifteen minutes passed before Gianna heard a gentle knock at the front door. She rushed to answer it.

Dr. Fornaro slipped in quickly. He banged his medical bag against the doorjamb and swore under his breath.

"Carmelina's upstairs," Gianna said. "I'll take you

up." She turned to shut the door, then froze.

Four German soldiers were coming around the corner. A lieutenant followed at their heels. The soldiers wore combat uniforms and carried rifles. The lieutenant held a big black pistol.

Gianna shut the door very quietly and locked it.

"What is it?" Dr. Fornaro hissed.

"Germans." Gianna began to tremble. It was a search party. They were going from house to house, hunting for men to take away.

She looked at Dr. Fornaro. He had turned pale. "Upstairs, quick," she said.

Her mother met them in the hall. "Doctor—"

"Mama, soldiers are coming," Gianna interrupted. "They're searching our street."

"Oh no." Mama covered her mouth. Her eyes grew big.

Gianna felt sick. If the search party had shown up an hour ago, it would have been all right. The soldiers might have stolen food, or taken Mama's ring, her last piece of jewelry. But they wouldn't have arrested Mama, Gianna, or Carmelina. A mother and two girls—one of them sick—were of no concern to the German army. But now Dr. Fornaro was here. He was in great danger.

There was no place to hide in the house. If there were, Papa and Uncle Luigi would have stayed.

"If the soldiers take Dr. Fornaro away, it'll be my fault," Gianna thought.

Dr. Fornaro sagged against the wall. He shook his head slowly, as if he'd already given up.

"We've got to do something," Gianna said.

Mama straightened her shoulders. "I know. He can hide under the bed. Dr. Fornaro, it'll be a tight squeeze, but—"

He shook his head again. "Don't you think the Germans know to look under beds?"

Gianna grabbed his hand. "No, not under the bed," she blurted. He was right: the Germans would know to look there. He needed a disguise. The Germans would surely arrest an old man, especially a doctor. A doctor was an important person. But they wouldn't arrest an old woman. That's why Signora Tozzano dared to keep watch out her window. "In the bed. Mama, quick: get an old nightgown and a *beretto da notte*." Gianna knew her mother kept one of the frilly caps in the clothes cupboard.

She pulled Dr. Fornaro up the hall to her own room and yanked the bedcovers down. Mama hurried in, carrying a long-sleeved nightgown and a *beretto da notte* trimmed in white lace.

"Do you think we can fool them?" Dr. Fornaro asked.

"I know we can," Gianna said. "Now hurry!"

Dr. Fornaro stripped off his jacket and kicked off his shoes. He rolled up his pant legs and shirt sleeves, then pulled the nightgown over his head. Gianna jammed the *beretto da notte* over his wispy hair, and he climbed into bed.

"Wait," Gianna said. She laid Dr. Fornaro's jacket, shoes, and medical bag on the bed beside him. The jacket and shoes could be easily concealed under the blanket, but the bag would make a lump. "Curl up around it," she said. The doctor turned on his side and clutched the bag to his stomach. Gianna pulled the covers up to the doctor's ears. "Good," she said. "You can't see it. Now remember: whatever happens, don't say a word."

Dr. Fornaro nodded. Just then, fists pounded on the front door. Mama gasped.

"Go back to Carmelina," Gianna said. "I'll let them in."

She ran downstairs. The pounding was thunderous. She quickly unlocked the door and threw it open.

The lieutenant stepped back, lowering his fist. His face was red with anger.

"There's nobody here but me and my mother and my little sister and my grandmother," Gianna blurted.

"We'll see," the lieutenant said. He spoke Italian with a thick accent, but Gianna could understand him. He stepped in, followed by the four soldiers.

"My little sister and my grandmother are very sick," Gianna said.

"Sick, h'm?" the lieutenant sniffed.

"Very sick," Gianna said.

The lieutenant said something in German, and the soldiers spread out to search the house. The lieutenant gestured to Gianna to go upstairs. He came after her, his boots clumping loudly on the steps.

She took him to her parents' room. Her mother was sitting beside Carmelina, who was moaning softly. The officer peered at Carmelina, and frowned.

"Where's your father?" he asked Gianna.

"Dead," she lied.

The officer frowned again. He stepped into the hall and pointed to a closed door. What's in there?"

"That's my grandmother's room," Gianna said. "She's sick, too."

The lieutenant flung the door open and peered in. From the doorway, Gianna saw Dr. Fornaro huddled under the covers. Only the top of his *beretta da notte* peeked out from beneath the blankets.

"H'm," the lieutenant said. He went back downstairs and barked at the soldiers. They shook their heads. He snapped an order and the men marched out of the house.

The lieutenant didn't even glance at Gianna as he left. She locked the door behind him, then raced upstairs. "They're gone!" she announced.

"Thank heaven," Dr. Fornaro said, stepping into the hall and tugging off the nightgown. "Now let me see what I can do for the little one."

Dr. Fornaro sent Gianna to fetch a basin of cool water. He poured some rubbing alcohol in the water, and washed Carmelina all over with the mixture. "That'll bring the fever down," he said. Then he took a small brown bottle from his bag. "We'll give her a teaspoon of this every four hours. She should be feeling better soon."

Dr. Fornaro sat up with Carmelina all night. At dawn, Carmelina's fever broke, and soon she was sitting up in bed eating a bowl of *farina*.

"I'd better get home," the doctor said. "I hope the Germans aren't early risers." He smiled as he left.

Two days passed with no more German raids. On the third morning—suddenly and wonderfully—Papa and Uncle Luigi came home.

"Papa!" Carmelina cried. He scooped her up and hugged her hard. Then he hugged Gianna and Mama. Uncle Luigi hugged everybody, too.

"Monte Cassino has fallen," Papa said. "The Germans are retreating."

"Is the war over?" Gianna asked.

"No." Papa's face darkened for a moment. "Not yet, *cara*. But the German soldiers are gone. We're safe." He kissed Mama tenderly. "Hungry, but safe."

"I'll get you some food," Mama said. "You must be starving." She looked at Gianna. "While I'm cooking, Gianna has quite a story to tell you."

"A story?" Papa asked.

"Gianna saved Carmelina's life," Mama said. "And Dr. Fornaro's"

Papa and Uncle Luigi stared at her.

Gianna smiled. She took Papa's hand, then reached for Uncle Luigi's, too. "Let's go in the kitchen," she said. "I'll tell you all about it."

Message
in the Music

AN ORIGINAL STORY BY
CAROL OTTOLENGHI-BARGA

Sally whacked the weeds growing around the old corn stalks with her short-handled hoe. Like the other slaves working in the fields, she'd wrapped a cloth around her head to keep off the blazing North Carolina sun.

Her little brother, Marcus, cut tobacco in the row on her right. He was only eight—really too young to be working in the field—but Sally liked keeping him close. She was thirteen, small but strong, and quick enough to help Marcus when he fell behind in his work.

William, the water boy, plodded by, singing softly. His song drifted to Sally on the wind.

> *Go down, Moses,*
> *way down in Egypt's land.*
> *Tol' old Pharaoh,*
> *let four o' my people go.*

Sally glanced over her shoulder. Samuel was harvesting near the road, keeping watch. He'd sing out if he saw the overseer coming, so it was safe to talk.

"Lizzie," Sally whispered to the woman on her left. "Those aren't the words to that song. What's William mean?"

Lizzie straightened and rubbed the small of her back. "You've got to listen, girl," she answered. "There's a message in the music. William says Miz Harriet Tubman freed four slaves last night. I heard the dogs baying, and I prayed those folks would escape. Sounds like they made it."

Sally shivered. "I wouldn't want to be caught by those dogs. Oh," she said when the water boy handed her a dipper, "many thanks, William."

He nodded, then said softly, "I hear tell the master plans to sell Marcus on Monday."

Sally's water splashed onto the ground. "He can't!"

she cried. "Marcus is the only family I have left." Sally's mama and baby sister had been sold last autumn. "If Marcus is sold, I'll be alone!"

"I'll still be with you, child," Lizzie said. She put her arm around Sally. "And I love you like my own. It'll tear my heart to see Marcus go, bad as when my Jessica was sold. But there's nothing we can do. A river of tears won't change the master's mind."

Angrily, Sally brushed tears from her cheeks. "You're right," she said. "Crying won't help. But Marcus can't be sold if he isn't here."

"What—" Lizzie started, but Samuel suddenly began singing loudly.

Michael, row the boat ashore, alleluia.
Michael, row the boat ashore, alleluia.
Sister help me tend the sail, alleluia.

The overseer was coming. Sally and Lizzie got back to work.

When the overseer blew his horn at quitting time, the slaves trudged back to their shacks. Sally leaned her hoe against the cabin she and Marcus shared with Lizzie. Like the other slave cabins, theirs was one room made of white-washed boards. It was raised off the ground on poles to keep snakes, bugs, and rainwater out. Three steps led to the only door. There was a shady spot behind the steps, underneath the cabin, where Sally liked to rest and think.

She crawled behind the steps now and stretched out on the cool dirt. She heard Marcus hooting with some other boys, trying to coax a sleepy barn owl from its roost. She heard adults splashing at the pump as they washed the dust from their arms and faces. The smell of burning pine logs, cornbread, and pork and beans drifted from the cookhouse.

"Thank heavens it's Saturday," she thought. "We don't have to go back to the field after dinner, or tomorrow, either. If we leave tonight, we might not be missed until Monday."

Sally lay under the cabin making plans until the bell rang for the evening meal. Then she hurried off to find Marcus.

"Don't eat your supper," she whispered to him as they stood in line. "Bring it to the cabin." She then carried her dish back to their cabin. Marcus followed.

"Why can't I eat?" Marcus asked as Sally took his food. "I'm hungry."

"You'll be hungrier later," Sally answered. She bundled the food and some water gourds into a blanket. "We're leaving."

"Won't we get a whipping?" Marcus asked fearfully.

"Only if we're caught."

The cabin door scraped open. Quickly Sally sat on the bundle, spreading her dress to cover it.

Lizzie slipped in. She gave Sally a gourd filled with cornbread and pork. "You'll need this," she said. "Do you children remember where the North Star is?"

Sally and Marcus nodded. Even the youngest slave could point out the North Star—it was the light that led folks to freedom.

"Good," Lizzie said. "Now, be careful. And Marcus, you mind your sister. Lord knows I'll miss you both, but you children have got to run." She gave both of them a quick kiss, then slipped out the door.

Sally tucked the gourd into the bundle. Then she peeked outside. Nearby, a woman sang as she took in laundry.

> *Sally, row the boat ashore, alleluia.*
> *Sally row the boat ashore, alleluia.*
> *Brother help her find the way, alleluia.*
> *Brother help her find the way, alleluia.*

Sally froze. The words to the song were different! Was there a message in this music, too? The woman glanced at Sally and nodded slightly, then picked up her washing and left.

What could "Sally, row the boat ashore" mean? Sally thought hard. Boats meant water. There was a river in the woods north of the cornfields. They'd have a better chance to escape if they stuck close to the river, Sally decided. Everyone said if you waded in the water, dogs couldn't track you.

Sally picked up her bundle and held her brother's hand as they crept into the darkening night. When they reached the cornfields, they ran through the rows of tall, yellow stalks until they reached the woods. Sally listened while they caught their breath.

"No one's chasing us yet," she said.

They followed first one path and then another deep into the woods. The night was dark and full of animal noises, but the children paid them no heed. Suddenly a shrill howl ripped through the air. And another. And another.

"Dogs," Sally said, her face grim. "Hurry."

Branches slapped their faces as they raced downhill. Marcus stumbled on a tree root. Sally grabbed his arm with one hand, clutched her bundle in the other, and kept running. The dogs' bawling grew louder, the howls now mixed with excited barks.

Sally could smell the dank green river now. But the dogs were gaining fast. She tore open the bundle and seized the gourd Lizzie had given them.

"Scatter this," she said, throwing the cornbread to Marcus. "Maybe it'll distract the dogs."

Marcus spread crumbs while Sally smeared the pork on the ground and wedged it under a boulder. Then she grabbed Marcus's hand and slid down the riverbank.

They gasped when they plunged into the cold water. Neither of them could swim, but Sally's tiptoes touched the river bottom. She held Marcus's head above water as they half-walked, half-floated down the river.

The howls behind them changed to confused yips and whines. Sally sighed in relief. The dogs had lost their scent.

Shivering, the children waded out of the water and wrung out their clothes as best they could. Then Sally took Marcus's hand. "We've got to find a clearing," she told him. "We can't see the North Star with all these trees blocking the sky, and the walking will warm us."

Marcus nodded, his teeth chattering.

They found a deer path that led to a tobacco field. Marcus spotted the North Star low on the horizon, and the children followed it until the stars began to fade.

"We'd better find someplace to hide," Sally said. "It'll be light soon."

Near a creek they found a hollow tree big enough for both of them to squeeze inside. Their blanket was still soaked from the river, but Sally hung it in front of the tree's opening to block the wind. Then they huddled together and fell asleep.

They woke up six hours later, cold and stiff.

Marcus coughed low and rumbly in his chest. "I'm hungry," he said. "and I'm still wet. I don't feel very good."

"You'll feel better after we eat," Sally said. She took his hand to pull him out of the hollow tree, then dropped it and felt his forehead.

"Oh no," she whispered. "Your hand is freezing, but your head is burning. I've got to get you warm before you catch pneumonia."

Sally covered him with leaves and set off. She didn't know where she was going, so every few steps she broke a branch or scraped the ground, marking her path back to Marcus.

Finally she came to a pigsty at the edge of a small farm. Sally crouched by the sty's split-rail fence. "Farms this size usually have only one or two slaves," she thought, "and they usually sleep in the house. Maybe Marcus and I could sneak into the barn when it gets dark. The animals would help keep us warm."

The pigs were making an awful racket. Sally peeked through the fence to see what was upsetting them. The sty was divided into two pens. A huge, grunting sow noisily gobbled food in one pen, while white-and-black piglets scampered and squealed in the other.

"Shoats," Sally thought with relief. "Old enough to leave their mama, but not big enough to be dangerous. They haven't been fed yet. If I hide until someone brings their slop, I can steal some for Marcus and me to eat."

"You're a runaway, ain't you?" whispered a voice.

Sally whirled around. A tall, light-brown girl stood over her. The girl held a battered metal bucket filled with table scraps and corn mush.

"No need to answer," the girl continued. She lifted the bucket and tipped it into the piglets' trough. "I know you are. You're not from around here—and anyway, no one hangs around a pigsty except runaway slaves and me. Runaways do because the smell keeps folks away, and there's always something to eat. I do because I feed the pigs."

Sally was about to run when the other girl grinned. "My name's Grace," she said. "And don't worry; I ain't going to turn you in. Someday I'm going to run away myself."

Grace banged her bucket against the trough. "Let the pigs keep their slop," she said. "I'll find you something fit to eat."

"Could I have some water, too?" Sally asked. "My brother caught a chill last night and has a fever."

Grace nodded. "It may take me a while," she said. "I've got work to do, and if I come back here right away it'll look funny. Put your brother in the shoats' pen. They're smelly, but their bodies'll warm him up. Stay hidden under the straw until you hear me singing."

Grace left, singing and banging her bucket against her knees loud enough to cover any noise Sally might make.

Sally raced to the hollow tree. She wasn't sure she could trust Grace, but Marcus was too sick to keep running, and she wasn't leaving him behind.

She half-carried, half-dragged Marcus to the pigsty. There she made a big nest of straw. She laid her brother in it, then piled some of the full, sleepy piglets on top of him. Marcus was so groggy from the fever that he didn't move, even when a piglet snuffled curiously in his face. Sally snuggled into the nest. She covered herself with straw, put her arms around Marcus, and waited to see what would happen.

Sally was so warm and so tired that she soon drifted off to sleep. She woke with a start when Grace sang out:

> *Didn't my Lord deliver Daniel,*
> *deliver Daniel, deliver Daniel?*
> *Didn't my Lord deliver Daniel?*
> *'N why not every child?*

Sally scrambled to her feet, disturbing a couple of the pigs. They grunted grumpily, then dozed off again.

"That looks cozy," Grace said, nodding her approval. She helped Sally lift Marcus's head so he could swallow a few sips of water. "You can stay here for a few days, till your brother's able to travel. Then some folks I know will help you to safety."

She handed Sally a gourd full of cold beans. The girls coaxed Macus into eating a few bites, then talked until Sally finished eating. Then Grace hurried back to the farmhouse.

Sally and Marcus stayed hidden. Grace brought them food and water twice a day when she fed the pigs.

Her visits were always short, so no one would wonder what she was up to.

Marcus's fever broke the second night at the farm, and he began to get better. On the fourth day, Sally woke up to see him pinching his nose shut.

"These pigs stink," he said.

Sally laughed quietly. "Now I'm sure you're getting better," she said. "Before you were too sick to complain. You should be grateful to these pigs—they saved your life."

"I didn't say I wasn't grateful," Marcus pointed out, "I said the pigs stink. And they do."

Grace was late that evening. Long after dark, she finally slipped into the pig pen.

"I can't stay," Grace whispered as she handed them some crumbling cornbread. "Slave catchers are at the house. They've been searching all the farms hereabouts."

"Are they looking for us?" Sally asked.

"They don't much care who they catch, long as they catch someone," Grace said. "Folks are ready to help you escape. You'll meet a man named Michael by the river, over thataway." She pointed east. "Right now, though, you've got to stay put."

She turned to leave. Sally touched her arm to stop

her. "I don't know what would have happened if you hadn't helped us," Sally said. "I think Marcus might've—"

"Don't think anything of it," Grace said, smiling. "Glad to do it. But now I've got to get back. Just be ready to go as soon as I give you a sign."

Early the next morning, Sally heard Grace's voice singing:

Swing low, sweet sailin' ship.
Comin' for to carry you home.
Swing low, it's time to go.
Comin' for to carry you home.

Sally smiled. "Thank you," she whispered into the breeze. She nudged Marcus. "Let's go. We're meeting someone named Michael who has a boat."

The children crept cautiously from the pigsty. Keeping low, they scurried east to the river. When they reached the riverbank, they peered around.

"Here," whispered a voice.

A thin black man paddled his canoe to the shore.

"I'm Michael," he said. "Grace said you were coming. Don't fret about the slave catchers. We'll keep you safe."

Sally and Marcus boarded the canoe. Michael paddled the canoe into a small branch of the river, then into a swamp. He steered them between the trees on one of the swamp's many water paths.

"Who's we?" Sally asked. "And why are we going into the swamp?"

Michael smiled. "This swamp makes a mighty safe hiding place for runaways," he said. "I've been here for several years, and some folks have been here longer than that. You can join our community if you like. Or you can rest up, and we'll help you head north."

"We could stay here?"

"Of course, child. There's no master here. You make your own decisions."

The canoe floated down another path. Suddenly an island loomed in front of them. Marcus clung to Sally's hand. "Where are we?" he asked.

Sally stared at the dozens of black men, women and children coming to greet them. She stared at the cabins, the vegetable plots, and the chickens and pigs running loose.

She hugged Marcus tight. "Home, Marcus," she said. "We're home." Then she started singing.

Swing low,
sweet sailin' ship.
Carryin' us to our new home.

Lily and the Darters

AN ORIGINAL STORY BY TIMOTHY TOCHER

Long ago, three orphaned sisters named Lily, Lilac and Lotus lived in a small village in southern China. Their parents had left them nothing but a rowboat from which Lily, the oldest, fished. The girls farmed rice in exchange for the shack in which to live.

During the growing season, the girls worked from dawn to dark. But in the winter, when there was little work to keep them busy, they longed for something more. Lily knew education could help them escape a life of drudgery.

Each winter the Ancient Master ran a school for

boys. The villagers often spoke of his fairness and wisdom, so Lily decided to approach him. One summer morning as he gazed at the glassy pond that bordered the village, Lily stood where he could see her and politely waited for him to speak.

"Young miss," he said at last, "Why are you not working on this fine morning?"

Lily bowed. "Ancient Master, my sisters and I respectfully ask permission to attend your school."

The Master raised one eyebrow in surprise. "My school is crowded," he said. "Boys take every available seat. These are boys who will someday lead the village and go out into the world to make their fortune. Why should I waste space on girls? Marry my students, and they will share as much of their knowledge as you need."

"We are as smart as any boys, sir, and need schooling just as much. My sisters and I are already on our own in the world. We have taught ourselves how to plant, tend, and harvest rice. Some of your students are still not trusted with a crop," answered Lily.

"Your presence would change my whole school, Lily. Soon other girls would ask to attend. To accept you, I need some proof of your intelligence," said the Ancient Master.

"What can we do to prove ourselves?" Lily asked.

"Do you see the dragonflies swooping around our heads? My students call them darters in honor of their great speed and dizzying acrobatics. For years I have offered a prize to anyone who can capture a darter without killing it. Boys have fallen in the pond, run into trees, and tripped over rocks chasing the darters, but none has succeeded. Prove you are smarter than the boys. For every live darter you bring me at the harvest festival, I will give you a seat in my school."

"But, sir, nature has made them uncatchable. How can we do what is impossible?"

"I will give you the same clue I give the boys, Lily: Use your head. Study the darters." Then the Ancient Master turned and left.

"How can I capture a darter?" Lily wondered as she sat down on the bank to watch their flight.

When Lily told her sisters about the challenge, Lilac and Lotus were eager to try. "Perhaps the three of us together can do what none of the boys could do alone," said Lotus.

Next morning the girls were at the pond to greet the sunrise. Lilac and Lotus waved branches at any darters that came near, trying to chase them toward

Lily and her waiting net. They raced around for a half-hour and never came close to a capture.

For several days, Lily watched the darters but made no further attempt to catch them. She noticed that they were all about the same size. She wondered why she never saw baby darters.

One morning the three girls were carrying buckets of water to the rice plants. The summer sun beat down on them and Lotus, the youngest, kept complaining about the heat. Lilac cooled her off by dumping a bucket of water on her head. Soon all three girls were splashing and laughing. Finally they collapsed on the ground, hugging each other and catching their breath.

When they got up to return to work, Lotus cried, "How heavy my clothes feel! It is hard even to walk."

This gave Lily an idea. "What if we soak the darters? Do you think they would still be able to fly if they were wet?"

"Haven't you given up yet?" asked Lotus.

"Do you want to go to school?" Lily asked her sisters. When they nodded, she said, "Then you must help me."

At dawn an eager Lily and her sleepy sisters were

standing on the shore of the pond, each holding a bucket of water. They formed a circle and threw water at any darter that flew inside it.

The darters dodged every drop of water and the girls only managed to soak each other. It was not fun being wet in the cool early morning. Lilac and Lotus sulked the rest of the day, but Lily was too busy thinking to notice.

Each evening Lily fished and studied the darters. She saw that even their mating was done in midair. Two darters would zoom around the pond locked in an embrace. The female would then dip down and lay her eggs in the murky water.

Suddenly a new idea popped into Lily's head. "That's it! The water!" Lily exulted. She rowed her boat to shore and raced home.

"Lilac! Lotus!" she called. "I need to use our boat to make a darter trap. Can we do without it until after the harvest festival?"

"How will you catch fish?" grumbled Lilac.

"I will fish from the bank, and we will make do with less. We may never again have a chance to go to school," said Lily.

"Let her have it," urged Lotus, "or we'll have no

peace. I wish the harvest were already here, so we could be done with this silliness."

Next evening, Lily rowed the boat to a secluded spot along the shore, then pulled it into the bushes. She stood the oars up in the oarlocks like twin masts. Then she used a bucket to shovel muck from the bottom of the pond into the boat.

Each scoop was full of tiny, squirming creatures that quickly burrowed out of sight. The muck smelled of rotting plants, but Lily worked on. She ladled pond water into the boat until it was almost full.

Then Lily took her fishing net, carefully undid its knots, and reknotted it into a net so fine that even an insect couldn't slip through the mesh. She drapped the net over the oars, then stretched it to form a roof over the rowboat. Next, she fastened the net to the sides of the boat. Finally, Lily stood back and admired her finished work. She hoped her idea was sound.

A week before the harvest festival, Lily visited the pond after a long day in the field. When she parted the bushes to examine her boat, she saw right away that something was different.

Grotesque little creatures were crawling all over the inside of the netting. Lily squatted close and watched.

The creatures hung from the net and twisted their bodies in a strange, silent dance.

As Lily watched, the creature nearest her twisted violently and split its back open. A new creature squeezed out through the opening, like a butterfly escaping from its cocoon. Lily felt an electric shock of joy.

The day of the harvest festival arrived. Lilac, Lotus, and Lily brushed their hair until it shone and put on their best clothing. In place of jewelry they wore wildflowers plaited around their necks and waists. Lily carried a small bamboo box.

The Ancient Master was seated beneath a shade tree enjoying a cup of rice wine. Fathers brought him samples of their crops. Mothers offered him their most savory dishes. All the parents hoped to gain admission to the Ancient Master's school for their sons.

Everyone stared when the three sisters approached. They stopped before the Master, Lily standing between Lilac and Lotus. All three bowed.

"Have you failed, Lily? I see no darters," the Master remarked.

Lily bowed again, then presented her box to him. He smiled and opened the lid. Dozens of darters burst out and zipped among the villagers like silent fireworks.

The crowd gasped in surprise when the Ancient Master rose and bowed to Lily. "Tell us, please, how you succeeded when so many boys failed." Ancient Master put a hand on Lily's shoulder and gently turned her to face the crowd.

"At first we foolishly raced around, chasing the darters as others had before," Lily said. Several of the boys hung their heads. "Then I remembered the Ancient Master's clue. I realized I'd have to use my head. Since I couldn't catch the adults, I captured the babies, which live in the pond. Then I waited for them to grow into darters."

"Lily and her sisters have proven that they deserve a chance to attend school," the Ancient Master announced. "I promised Lily one seat for each darter she captured, so it seems she is entitled to my whole classroom."

"Thank you, Ancient Master," Lily responded. "I want only three seats—for myself and my sisters. Let the other darters save places for girls in future years who wish to attend."

And from that day forth the Ancient Master opened his school to anyone who showed a love for learning.

Samantha's Dog-Gone Adventure

An Original Story by Kelli Marlow Allison

Latin Word:
Pro bono (pronounced "pro BO-no"): something done for free, for the public good.

Samantha Applegate reached Elm Street, the end of her paper route, exactly on schedule. When she braked her bike at Mr. Hardison's driveway, Duke barked a hello. The German shepherd trotted to her, his tail wagging and his orange collar and silver tags shining in the sun. "Hi there, fella; here's your paper," Samantha said.

Samantha walked her bike to the house next door. Granny Goodman sat in her creaking porch swing. As Samantha came up the drive, Granny peered over her half-glasses and smiled. Samantha always brought Granny's paper to her front door.

"Good morning, Samantha. I baked some chocolate-chip cookies for you." Granny held up a brown paper sack. "Fluffy, I know you're glad to see Samantha, but settle down," she told the big white cat dancing figure eights around Samantha's legs. "I baked a double batch, so there's plenty for you and your mom." Granny handed the plump sack to Samantha.

"Mmm . . . they smell so chocolatey!" Samantha hugged Granny's neck. "We'll have a feast!" Samantha picked up Fluffy and scratched her chin. "Do you need anything from the store? I could stop by after school."

"Bless you, child." Granny shook her head. "Can't think of a thing. You'd better take off. I don't want to make you late for school."

Granny was Samantha's last customer on this side of the block. At the end of Granny's driveway, she waited to cross the street as an unfamiliar pickup truck slowly cruised by from the direction of Mr. Hardison's house. It continued down Elm Street and stopped in front of an old house that had been vacant for over a year. It was the last house on Elm Street and sat beside a large wooded area with a creek running through it. Samantha made a mental note to ask the new tenants if they needed paper delivery.

When Samantha returned home, she plopped the sack of cookies on the kitchen counter and slid into her seat at the breakfast table. "Granny sent cookies for lunch, Mom."

Her mother poured herself a cup of coffee, sat down, and pulled a sheaf of legal files from her briefcase. "That's something to look forward to," she said absentmindedly.

Samantha munched cornflakes and speed-read the front page of the newspaper. Samantha's teacher gave pop quizzes on current events right after the morning bell. The student who gave the best two-minute rundown of any unusual news event earned extra credit. Samantha had a running battle going with Herman Horvath to get the most credits.

Samantha loved anything with wings, fins, or fur. The woes of any animal—from a spotted owl in Oregon to a whale off Maine—always won her sympathy. Today her eyes zeroed in on a picture directly under a headline screaming: "DOG SENTENCED TO DIE!"

"Look at that adorable face!" Samantha exclaimed. She skimmed the article and showed the newspaper to her mother. "Mom, you can't let them kill that poor, defenseless dog!"

Her mother looked up from her files. "You're just like me: always rooting for the underdog—pardon the expression."

Samantha made a face. "Mom, you're a lawyer, not a comedian. That dog needs help, not lame jokes! Listen to this," Samantha said as she read the article. "'Behind the gray bars of doggie death row sits a mixed-breed named Jumbles, tried and convicted of biting a man but granted a stay of execution while Mr. Purdue, his homeless owner, appeals.'"

Her mother took the paper from Samantha. "It seems Jumbles attacked a Mr. Olson." She turned the page. "Here's a picture of Olson. Look at that handlebar mustache. I haven't seen one like that in years." She read the article, interested now. "Mr. Olson says he's a traveling salesman. H'm, I wonder why he was outside after midnight."

Samantha pleaded, "Mom, you have to help Jumbles. You could represent Mr. Purdue. Since he's homeless, he can't afford to hire a lawyer. I've heard you say your firm does *pro bono* work for worthwhile causes." Samantha leaned over her mother's shoulder. "Jumbles's face is so gentle."

Her mother picked up her briefcase. "What are we going to do about Jumbles?" Samantha persisted.

"*We* aren't going to do anything. You are going to make tracks down the driveway before you miss the bus, and I am going to court. This afternoon I'll make a few phone calls. Mind you, I'm only saying I'll look into it. I haven't promised I'll do anything."

In the week that followed, Samantha's mother had several talks with Mr. Purdue and became convinced Jumbles deserved to go free. She decided that Mr. Purdue's case was worthy enough to take *pro bono*.

Samantha, who had already given her rundown on Jumbles to her class, kept them posted as the case progressed toward a court date. She explained to them that the exact Latin term used in legal documents is *pro bono publico,* which means "for the public good," and that in such cases lawyers represent a client without pay.

A week later, Samantha sat in the courtroom and watched her mom defend Jumbles's owner. Samantha stared at Mr. Purdue, trying to decide what kind of man he was. He had obviously spruced up for court. He'd neatly combed his thinning hair and his face sported shaving nicks. Samantha had never seen a face so wrinkly. It reminded her of an old purse of Mom's she'd played with when she was little. Still, it was a kindly face with bright, honest eyes. Samantha nodded to herself. Mr. Purdue had a face she'd trust.

Then Samantha glanced over at Mr. Olson. She recognized his handlebar mustache from the newspaper picture. "It makes him look pompous and mean," she thought.

Her mother was questioning Mr. Purdue. "Tell us in your own words, Mr. Purdue: why did Jumbles bite Mr. Olson?"

"Well, since I was sleeping, I'm not real sure what started things off, but I know Mr. Olson was holding my radio when I woke up. And some other guy was messing with Daisy—that's Jumbles's girlfriend—and her puppies. Daisy got real nervous cuz her pups are only two weeks old. She started growling, and Jumbles snapped at Mr. Olson."

Mr. Purdue fidgeted and looked down at his feet. "It was all pretty confusing. Mr. Olson claims there ain't no other guy, that I must've been dreaming. He says he was just out for a walk when Jumbles jumped him. Says he never touched my radio." Straightening his shoulders, Mr. Purdue's voice grew stronger. He looked directly at the judge. "But I'm telling you the gospel truth, Your Honor. Jumbles is a good dog. He wouldn't attack nobody without a reason. I swear my radio was in that man's hands when I woke up! That part I am sure of."

"Thank you, Mr. Purdue. You may step down," Samantha's mother said. Turning to the judge, she said, "Your Honor, while Mr. Purdue is homeless, he is still entitled to protect his property. That property includes his dogs, Jumbles and Daisy, and their puppies, as well as the radio Mr. Olson was trying to steal."

She walked toward the judge holding Jumbles's picture. "Jumbles attacked Mr. Olson after—and only after—Mr. Olson attempted to steal Mr. Purdue's radio and his accomplice attempted to steal Daisy's puppies. Jumbles was justified in protecting his master's property, including his own puppies!"

"Mrs. Applegate," the judge said, "I will give your appeal serious thought. You will have my decision tomorrow." The judge banged the gavel. "Court is adjourned."

Samantha's mother guided Mr. Purdue to where

Samantha sat and introduced them. Samantha looked up at the stoop-shouldered man smiling down at her, his faded blue eyes twinkling, and put her hand out. "I'm sure you'll get Jumbles back," she said.

Mr. Purdue shook her hand gravely. "I've got a lot of faith in your ma. But I've got to thank you, too. Your mother says it was you who talked her into taking my case."

"It's nice to meet you, Mr. Purdue," said Samantha. Then she said to her mother, "Mom, I've got to run. It's time to collect payments for my papers."

Samantha's mother told Mr. Purdue, "Samantha has a paper route to earn money for college. She wants to be a lawyer."

Mr. Purdue winked at Samantha. "If she's anything like her ma, she'll be great."

A couple of hours later, Samantha finished her collections. As she left her last customer, she remembered that she still hadn't checked on the new tenants in the house at the end of Elm Street. Looking down the street, she saw a man open the front door of the house as another man carrying a blanket-wrapped package came out and scuttled into the driver's seat of a pickup. The man's face was turned away, but his outline reminded Samantha of Mr. Olson. As the pickup sped by, she stared at its driver—it was Mr. Olson. Meanwhile, the other man went back into the house and slammed the door.

Samantha biked to the shabby two-story house. Giant elms hid its roof, and a dim light outlined closed shades in the front windows. Samantha went to the door and rang the bell. No answer.

"That's funny," Samantha muttered. She knew someone was inside; she'd seen him go inside. Samantha circled the house and knocked on the side door. Still no answer. Curious, Samantha scanned the backyard. Nothing. As she was about to leave, she caught a glimpse of something bright in the grass. Samantha leaned over the backyard fence and squinted her eyes. She could make out an orange strap and a glint of silver.

"H'm," Samantha thought. "I could be wrong, but that looks like Duke's collar! How weird. What can that be doing here?" With a frown, Samantha reluctantly left.

At supper Samantha told her mother about the strange happenings on Elm Street. As they puzzled over the events, the phone rang.

Samantha answered the phone, then returned to

the table. "That was Granny Goodman. She wanted to know if I'd seen Fluffy this afternoon. Fluffy didn't come home for dinner."

"Duke probably chased her up a tree," her mother said.

Samantha shook her head. "Granny checked with Mr. Hardison. He said Duke has disappeared, too." Samantha's brow furrowed. She was sure that was Duke's collar she'd seen.

As Samantha loaded the dishwasher, she remembered Mr. Olson's pickup cruising slowly past Mr. Hardison's house a week ago. That memory triggered another—of a current-events article she'd read for school last month. The *State News* had reported numerous missing German shepherds in the area. Dognappers were transporting them east, where schools for the blind paid top dollar for German shepherds because they made excellent guide dogs. The article had said one of the ringleaders was still at large.

"Mom," Samantha said, "What kind of dog is Daisy?"

Her mother looked puzzled. "I have no idea. I only know Jumbles is a mixed breed. That's where his name comes from—he's a jumble of husky, German shepherd, and collie."

"I'll bet Daisy is a German shepherd," Samantha said. "What difference does it make?"

"Because Duke is a German shepherd!" Samantha crowed excitedly.

"Samantha, you're not making sense." Her mother frowned. "Mr. Purdue and Mr. Hardison don't even know each other. I don't see any connection between them—or their dogs."

"We've got to rescue Duke! Mr. Olson is a dognapper! His friend was trying to steal Daisy's pups while Olson kept Jumbles busy. They didn't count on Mr. Purdue waking up. We've got to call the police!"

"Slow down." Samantha's mother grasped her agitated daughter by the shoulders. "Calm down and tell me what's going on."

Samantha's mother listened carefully as Samantha described the pieces of the puzzle. Then she nodded thoughtfully, picked up the phone, and dialed 911.

Twenty minutes later Samantha and her mother waited across the street from Mr. Olson's house. The pickup was parked in front of the house again, so Samantha guessed Mr. Olson had returned home. They watched as the police knocked on the door.

"Open up," one of the officers shouted. "It's the

police. We'd like to ask you a few questions."

Samantha saw a shade rise and fall in an upstairs window. A few moments later, Mr. Olson opened the door a crack, leaving the chain on.

"What's going on?" he asked gruffly.

"A number of people in this area have reported missing pets," explained the officer. "So we are checking with everyone in the neighborhood to see if they've had any problems. Do you have pets?"

"No," he mumbled, "not me. I have no use for pets."

Just as he said that, the police heard a muted yelp.

"Now that's interesting," said the police officer. "You did say you had no pets, didn't you?"

"Well...I..." Mr. Olson looked scared.

"If you don't mind," the officer said with a friendly smile, "we'd like to have a look around. May we?"

Samantha saw Mr. Olson's shoulders fall. He closed the door to remove the chain, opened it again, and gestured the police into the house.

"You might as well," he said.

Samantha had been holding her breath during the whole exchange. Her heart thumped anxiously as the officers disappeared inside. She finally relaxed when one of the officers led five muzzled dogs out of the house.

"Duke!" she yelled, running toward one of the dogs. "You're all right!"

The police officer handed Duke over to Samantha's mother, saying, "I'm sorry, Mrs. Applegate, but we didn't find any cats in the house. Since you know this dog, would you mind taking him to his owner? We'll take care of the rest."

As the officer spoke, other officers led Mr. Olson and his partner outside. They were handcuffed and placed in the backseat of a police car.

Samantha and her mother took Duke to Mr. Hardison's house. Mr. Hardison was overjoyed.

Samantha was still worried about Fluffy. "Where could she be?" she wondered. "Could there be catnappers on the loose, too?" Then Samantha noticed that Duke's feet were caked in mud. She snapped her fingers. "Let's go look in the woods. I bet Duke's been in the creek recently. Maybe he was chasing Fluffy."

When the trio started for the woods, Duke raced to a towering oak and started barking. From high overhead came a forlorn mewing. Fluffy clung midway up the tree. Samantha climbed up and brought Fluffy down. She cuddled the trembling cat and headed straight for Granny's house.

The next day in the courtroom, Samantha listened as a police officer told the judge about Mr. Olson's dognapping activities. The officer concluded by saying, "Thanks to Miss Samantha Applegate, we'll be able to put an end to dognapping throughout the state." The judge immediately ordered Jumbles released.

Later, at the pound, tears filled Samantha's eyes as she watched Mr. Purdue hug Jumbles.

"This is a dog-gone happy ending," her mother said.

Samantha scowled. "Mom, must you?"

Mr. Purdue winked at Samantha. "Me and Jumbles are gonna skedaddle. Dog jokes are as contagious as fleas, and I don't aim to catch 'em!"

Grinning from ear to ear, Samantha gave a victorious whoop and hugged her mother. Just then a camera flashed, and a man hurried toward them. "I write for the *State News*. May I ask you some questions?"

Samantha hugged her mother again. "Maybe my teacher will give me double points for *being* a current event. Then Herman will never catch up to me!"

Chita's Garden

AN ORIGINAL STORY BY DIANE SAWYER

Spanish Words:
Bueno (pronounced "BWE-no"): means "good."
Finca (pronounced "FEEN-ka"): a ranch or farm.
Güisquil (pronounced "gwess-KEEL"): a kind of squash.

Chita knelt in her tiny yard, savoring the shade beneath the tall leafy banana plants. She scooped up handfuls of corn kernels from her woven mat and sifted them between her fingers. *Bueno*! The kernels were sun-dried and ready for grinding.

Chita tossed her thick black braid over her shoulder and spread a handful of kernels across a flat grinding stone. Humming a tune passed down from her Mayan ancestors, she grasped the ends of a cylindrical stone and rolled it back and forth across the other stone, crushing the corn. From time to time—as the sun rose higher and higher—Chita gazed at the hills above the adobe houses of her village of Magdalena Milpas. The hills shone beautifully as they slowly emerged from the early-morning clouds of the Guatemalan highlands.

Chita smiled. The corn kernels were turning into golden mounds of flour. Her mouth watered, already relishing the delicious tortillas she and Mami would prepare for the midday meal.

As she finished grinding the corn, Chita's eyes turned to her family's garden. The rows of corn, tassels shimmering in the sunshine, filled Chita with pride. Corn had sustained her ancestors for thousands of years. Her village, Magdalena Milpas, was even named after corn— "milpas" was the Mayan word for cornfields.

Now that Chita was twelve, the garden was her responsibility. She weeded, hoed, and picked the corn that fed Papi, Mami, and her older brothers, Luis and Felipe. She made use of every inch of soil behind her house by planting squash between the corn rows and beans along the garden's edges.

"Chita!" Mami called from the doorway. "Please

start the fire. Papi and the boys will be back soon."

Chita brushed the bits of corn from her colorful skirt and white blouse. Her fingertips lingered on the purple flowers that Mami had embroidered along the blouse's neckline. If only she could weave and embroider like Mami. But she had no talent for fancy work. Helping Papi weave sleeping mats from cornhusks— that was her only handicraft. Chita sighed and lit the scraggly pile of firewood.

Mami knelt next to Chita and placed her water jug between them. "We will have a special treat with our tortillas today," she said as she mixed the corn flour with water. "Papi's favorite . . . *güisquil.*" She nodded toward the bowl of cut-up squash she would wrap with banana leaves and bake over the fire.

Chita knew that Mami was trying to be cheerful. The *fincas* where Papi and most of the village men worked were closed because bad weather had ruined the coffee crop. The layoffs were supposed to be temporary, but the weeks without work had stretched into months and now no one knew when they would end.

"Mami, I'm sure there will be good news from the *fincas* today," Chita said.

Mami frowned and said nothing. She and Chita

shaped and patted the corn-paste dough into tortillas. Chita saw tears running down her mother's cheeks. "Mami, what's wrong?"

"Several families are leaving our village to go to Antigua. They hope to find work in the factories there." Mami sobbed. "Papi thinks we should go, too."

"But this is our home!" Chita said proudly. "We can't leave! We are Maya-Quiché Indians! We will remain here where our ancestors grew their corn."

Mami wiped away her tears. "Don't talk such foolishness. Without the money Papi and the boys earn on the *fincas*, we can't buy wool and cotton for me to weave into fabric. Without fabric to sell at the market, there is no money to buy firewood to cook our meals. Papi and the boys must spend all morning near Lake Atitlán searching for firewood. This is a bad circle with no end. Papi is right. We must move to the city."

Mami's words cut deep, like a machete. There had to be another solution. But the more Chita thought about the problem, the worse the situation seemed. Mami nudged Chita. "We cannot waste our firewood," she said. "Stop staring into the flames and put them to good use."

Embarrassed at her thoughtlessness, Chita placed several tortillas on a clay disk and set the disk over the fire to bake. Still, Chita couldn't stop thinking about her family's predicament. She didn't want to move away from her home.

"Papi and the boys are home," Mami said. "They must be starved."

Chita looked up and saw Papi, Luis, and Felipe. She could tell from their grim expressions that their pile of firewood was even smaller than yesterday's. Papi forced a smile and patted Chita on the head. "Mmm-mmm. Smells good." He licked his lips. "I've been tasting baked *güisquil* all the way from Lake Atitlán."

Felipe rubbed his hand across his shirt and flat stomach. "I could eat those tortillas all by myself," he said. Luis agreed. "Let's eat," he said.

As they pulled their mats into a circle, Papi said, "I have come to a painful decision." His fingers nervously smoothed his sash. "With the *fincas* closed, none of us can find any work. We will leave Magdalena Milpas on Monday morning, three days from now."

Chita fought the lump in her throat. She would not cry. She would be brave, like her brothers and parents. After the family had finished eating, Papi and the boys returned to Lake Atitlán. They would canoe to the deep waters and catch fish for the evening meal.

Chita and Mami began husking the corn that Chita had picked early that morning. "We'll dry the kernels in the sun and take them with us to the city," Mami said, already resigned to her fate.

Chita pushed aside the cornhusks. "I wish I were a little girl again. I would take out my basket of worry dolls." She closed her eyes and remembered the six dolls, each one smaller than her pinky. They were made of twigs wrapped with colorful thread and they had painted faces. "I would tell them our family's problems and—tzu-tzu-tzu—our worries would disappear."

All at once, Chita's face lit up. "Mami, I will sell worry dolls at the market! Isn't that a good idea?"

Mami shook her head. "There are too many worry dolls at the market. They won't sell. You know how tourists are. They always want something different."

Chita lowered her head and continued to husk the corn. As she worked, a breeze ruffled the pile of corn, making the green, leafy husks look like they were alive. "Look, Mami. The corn's dancing. See—the husks look like twirling skirts." Chita smoothed a husk fragment with her fingertips. "A doll's skirt." Chita's eyes sparkled. She scooped up several cornhusks. "Mami, could I make a doll from cornhusks?"

"Stop your foolishness and help me husk the corn." Mami's voice crackled with impatience.

"Please, Mami?" Chita pleaded. "I have an idea."

"Quickly," Mama said and continued husking.

Chita grabbed a pile of discarded cornhusks, shook them out, then tried to twist and tie them into different shapes. But the green cornhusks were too slippery and each knot she attempted fell apart. She scooped up several dried cornhusks from the piles that she and Papi had set aside to weave into sleeping mats. She folded a dried cornhusk into a small oval and tied a string inside it.

"The head," she explained to Mami. She worked quickly, adding and tying off cornhusks to make different parts of the doll—the body, the arms, and finally the legs. Chita wove all of the parts together with string. After tying off the wrists and waist, she held up the plump doll, proud of her creation.

"Well?" Chita smiled. "What do you think?"

Mami scoffed. "You're too old for dolls."

"It's to sell at the market."

Mami shook her head. "Who would buy such a plain doll?"

Chita sighed. She gazed absentmindedly across her

tiny yard and noticed the dried corn kernels that had fallen near the grinding stones. In the bright sunshine, they glistened like gold.

Chita dashed into the house. She returned with Mami's embroidery thread and needle. She pierced the corn kernels, strung them onto the thread, and draped the kernels around the doll's neck.

Mami smiled. "*Bueno.* A necklace."

"I will make the doll even more beautiful," Chita said. She quickly fashioned corn-kernel earrings and bracelets. She embroidered eyes, a nose, and a mouth on the doll's face.

"Hair," Chita said enthusiastically. "She will be prettier with hair." She gathered the golden corn tassels and sewed them onto the doll's head.

"Mami, my doll needs a skirt and blouse."

"We have no cloth, only the clothes on our backs and the spare set for when we wash these."

"What about my new skirt and blouse in the cupboard? They were your birthday present to me."

Chita knew that Mami had spent long hours weaving the cloth and sewing. The skirt and blouse were the prettiest and most colorful she had ever owned. Chita was saving them for a special occasion.

Chita ran into the house and returned gripping a pair of scissors and carrying her new skirt and blouse.

"Stop!" Mami gasped, rising to her feet.

But it was too late. Snip! Snip! Chita slit her skirt. Snip! Snip! Chita cut her blouse. Tears rolled down Mami's cheeks but it was too late to stop Chita. Soon she had fabric for twelve skirts and blouses.

Mami composed herself. "You are making a big sacrifice to keep our family here. I will help you." She unwound her red headwrap and pressed it into Chita's hands. "Your dolls must have headwraps."

Chita threw her arms around Mami. "My dolls will remind tourists of their trip to Magdalena Milpas."

Mami slid her embroidery needle into the blouse fabric. "It is our last hope," she said sadly. Chita thanked Mami, then she turned to the cornhusks and began making more dolls. When Papi and the boys returned, Papi said, "What have we here, a little factory?"

Papi held up one of the dolls. "A genuine Milpas doll," he said. His dark eyes shone with admiration. "My grandmother used to make dolls like this when she was a child."

Chita said, "Mami and I will sell them at the market on Sunday and buy firewood with our earnings." Her voice rose with excitement. "And wool and cotton. Maybe we can sell enough to last us until the *fincas* begin hiring again."

Papi said, "I will help. Mami, where shall I begin?"

"You must ask Chita," Mami said. "It is her factory."

Chita pointed at the dried cornhusks. "Papi, please set them into piles of twelve."

Felipe said, "I'll gather tassels for the dolls' hair."

Luis chimed in, "I'll get corn for their jewelry."

Chita and her family worked that afternoon and all the next day. Sunday morning, while Papi and the boys picked corn, Chita and Mami wrapped the dolls in a big blanket and walked to the market. Chita gnawed her lip as they set up the dolls to sell. "What if no one bought the dolls?" she thought.

She soon found she had nothing to worry about. Talk of the authentic Milpas dolls quickly spread among the tourists. Everyone had to have the symbol of Milpas, a true Mayan corn doll.

"We can stay in our home," Mami said joyfully as she sold the last doll.

"The corn saved us," Chita said.

"No," Mami said, hugging Chita. "Your hard work and quick thinking saved us."

Shannon Holmes's First Case

AN ORIGINAL STORY BY STEPHEN MOOSER

In all my thirteen years, I'd never seen the streets of London so full of fine carriages. Like me, all the Londoners were on their way to the Royal Stakes horse race at Ascot Park.

My uncle, the famous detective Sherlock Holmes, had invited me to share a carriage ride to the races. It was to be a very special occasion for my school, Essex Academy. The Academy had burned to the ground just months earlier. Our good friend Sir William Vickers had pledged to help rebuild it with proceeds from a victory today by his horse, Incredible Start.

I never tired of my uncle's tales about the many mysteries he'd solved. His ability to coax clues out of the flimsiest scraps of evidence was legendary. Someday I hoped to follow in his fabled footsteps.

As we stepped from the carriage at Ascot Park, I couldn't help noticing that my uncle was drawing thoughtfully on his pipe, his mind miles away. He had been distracted a lot lately. A robbery at one of London's largest banks had been perplexing him for weeks.

As we made our way through the crowd, my uncle tipped his tweed hat to a distinguished-looking man in a long coat, then smiled at half a dozen others. Uncle Sherlock might have been better known than the Lord Mayor himself. He usually attended events like this with his assistant, Dr. Watson, but today he had invited me. I told him I considered it a singular honor.

"The honor is all mine," he remarked, patting me on the shoulder. "Though I've not been blessed with children, I think of you as my own daughter."

We strolled through a tunnel beneath the grandstand and emerged onto a fenced lawn. Beyond the fence lay the track.

"There he is: Incredible Start," said Uncle Sherlock. "A magnificent horse, don't you think?"

I had to agree. Incredible Start was a stunning horse: black as coal and swift as the night train to Southhampton, folks said. Sir William Vickers was standing alongside Incredible Start while his jockey carefully brushed the horse's shimmering mane.

"Sir William!" called Uncle Sherlock, waving his cap. "Good luck!"

When Sir William saw my uncle, he signaled for us to enter the paddock through a nearby gate.

"So glad you could come," said Sir William, reaching out for my uncle's hand, then mine. "We'll soon have that academy of yours filled with scholars. Won't we, Miss Shannon?"

I curtsied. "You are very generous," I said.

"I owe my success to my education," said Sir William. "Rebuilding your school is the least I can do to repay the favor."

"It doesn't take a detective to figure out who will win today's contest," said Uncle Sherlock. He patted Incredible Start on the shoulder. "It's elementary. Your horse will do as he always does—win by ten lengths."

Sir William sighed. "I thought so myself before this afternoon," he said, "but there's been a surprise. A horse called Midnight Star was entered by a man you know well: Henry Bonner."

"Bonner!" said Uncle Sherlock. "Why, that's the scalawag I helped put in jail last year for flimflamming the city's carriage operators."

"He's little better than a pirate," I said, recalling how he'd promised many of the drivers accident insurance, taken their deposits, then tried to skip town.

"He's free already?" asked Uncle Sherlock.

"Released on good behavior," said Sir William. He snorted. "Can you believe it? Now here he is with one of the finest thoroughbreds I've ever seen."

Midnight Star was not hard to spot. He matched Incredible Start in nearly every aspect, from his inky coloring to his muscled haunches. The only difference was a white mark on his forehead.

Mr. Bonner, a man with a drooping red mustache and a shiny black top hat, stood beside his horse. He was talking to his jockey.

"Solved the Baron's Bank case yet?" asked Sir William, changing the subject. "Imagine: someone just walked into that vault, picked up a bag of money, and strolled out. Why didn't anyone see the thief?"

Uncle Sherlock shook his head. "It is most baffling. The thief must work for the bank, but who is it? Every employee has a solid alibi."

"Is the crime unsolvable then?" asked Sir William.

"On the contrary," said Uncle Sherlock. "A piece of the puzzle is missing, but it will turn up. It always does."

"Perhaps the thief was disguised as an employee," I suggested quietly.

"An intriguing possibility," said Uncle Sherlock. He tipped his cap at me. "I like the way your mind works."

I beamed at my uncle's compliment. "Keep at it, Shannon," he continued, "and soon there will be a new S. Holmes making life miserable for the city's criminals."

"One Holmes is already too many," a gruff voice interrupted. I looked up and caught the bloodshot eyes of Henry Bonner, who was holding his horse by the bridle and glaring at my uncle.

"If you don't mind, we were talking to Sir William," said my uncle coolly.

Bonner sneered. "If you're smart, Sir William, you'll spare yourself some humiliation today. Midnight Star will leave your nag in the dust."

"I don't believe I've ever heard of Midnight Star,"

said Sir William. "Where has he raced?"

"Morocco, primarily," said Bonner. "I purchased him from a wealthy sheik." He nodded. "Believe me. He's the genuine article."

"I have no reason to doubt you," said Sir William, ever the gentleman. Midnight Star nuzzled my neck. I ran my hand gently across the mark on his forehead.

"Morocco," I whispered into his ear. "Such a long way from home!"

I smiled and stepped away just as the trumpeters announced the Royal Stakes with a blast of their horns.

"Neeeayyy!"

Incredible Start reared up on his hind legs, startled. I jumped back, barely avoiding his flailing hooves. As his shoes flashed by, I noted that they were well worn.

"Steady, steady," said Sir William's jockey, clasping the bridle tightly. "Sorry, sir. He's been jumpy all day."

"He has good reason to be nervous," said Bonner as he led Midnight Star toward the track. "This could very well be his last race."

I watched Midnight Star walk away, his polished shoes reflecting the sun. He seemed like such a nice horse. It was a shame he raced for such an awful man.

"Well," said my uncle, turning back to Sir William.

"We won't keep you any longer. We're anxious to see Incredible Start cross the finish line for Essex Academy."

"He'll cross the line," said Sir William. "Let's just hope it's in first place. Bonner has a very special thoroughbred there. Don't count your money yet."

"We'll be cheering for you," said my uncle. Sir William nodded, then helped his jockey into the saddle and led Incredible Start away.

"There's something wrong with that horse," said Uncle Sherlock as we left the paddock. "Did you see the way he reared up?"

"I couldn't help but notice," I said, hiking up my dress as we climbed to a spot with a clear view of the track. I shaded my eyes with my hand and crinkled my nose. Something smelled! The odor reminded me of the Union Jack Laundry on Beckworthy Street.

I turned my attention to the upcoming race. While the huge crowd chatted excitedly, we watched the horses take their positions in the starting gate. The Royal Stakes was one full lap of the track, with the finish immediately in front of the grandstand.

Incredible Start took the inside post and Midnight Star the outside. Once locked into the gate the twelve horses shifted anxiously in their stalls as they waited for the doors to spring open and the race to begin.

"No one can catch Sir William's horse," said Uncle Sherlock. "He usually starts slow, but he's got the inside post and blinding speed."

I hoped my uncle was correct. Essex Academy depended on it. Suddenly a tiny flag flipped up atop the starting gate. BRRRRING! The stall doors flew open and the horses bolted onto the track.

"They're off!" yelled a red-faced man beside me. He pumped his fist in the air. "Go! Go! Go!"

Incredible Start burst from the gate like a scared rabbit and led for the first few steps. Midnight Star came out of the gate last, but he quickly caught up, sliced across the track to the rail, and grabbed the lead. The noise from the crowd was deafening. All the spectators were screaming for their horses to catch Midnight Star. I'd only attended a few races in my life, but I knew enough to see that nobody, including Incredible Start, was going to catch Midnight Star.

"Sir William's horse is finished," said Uncle Sherlock. He shook his head. "Midnight Star looks more like Incredible Start than Incredible Start himself."

I shaded my eyes again to get a better look at the horses. Once again I smelled something that reminded me of a laundry. The smell, along with my uncle's words, made something click in my head.

"More like Incredible Start than Incredible Start himself," I shouted. My words were lost in the roar of the crowd as the horses rounded the far turn and came thundering down the homestretch.

"Blast it all!" screamed the red-faced man as Midnight Star crossed the finish line ten lengths ahead of the others. Incredible Start crossed the line thirty lengths back, accompanied by jeers from the crowd.

"Sometimes even a sure thing isn't sure," said my uncle. He squeezed my shoulder gently. "I'm sorry about your school."

"The race isn't over," I said. My uncle glanced at the track, then turned and studied me.

"But the race is over," he said. "Have you seen something I missed?"

"Perhaps it's nothing," I said. "But do you remember when Incredible Start reared up?"

"Of course."

"His shoes looked worn," I said, "as if he'd spent more time on the streets than on the track."

"Curious," said my uncle.

"Very curious," I said. "Do you know when Sir

William bought Incredible Start?"

"Two years ago, I believe," said Sherlock.

"And the horse was already named Incredible Start, I presume," I said.

"We'll have to ask Sir William himself," said my uncle. "Here he comes now. Sir William!"

Sir William had gone out onto the track to console his jockey. He now was walking back with Incredible Start. Sir William looked up and forced a smile.

"Sorry, Shannon. He just didn't have it today. Tough luck, I guess."

"I'm not so certain," I said. "Tell me, who named your horse?"

Sir William stopped at the rail. "His previous owner, I believe. Why do you ask?"

"My uncle told me he usually starts slow," I said. "If he is slow to start, why is he named Incredible Start?"

"Where is this leading?" asked my uncle.

"I think his name comes not from the way he races, but the way he was born," I said. I turned back to Sir William. "In school I learned that identical twins are rare among horses."

"It's true," said Sir William.

My uncle chewed on his pipe. "An interesting line

of inquiry," he said. "Shannon, I believe you are on to something here. I suggest we pay Mr. Bonner a visit."

In short order the three of us were standing in the winner's circle, just off the track, watching a half-dozen officials congratulate Henry Bonner. Just as a tall gentleman in a purple coat was handing him a silver trophy and the prize money, I cleared my throat loudly.

"You're awarding the trophy to the wrong man," I said. "The horse that won the race belongs to Sir William Vickers."

Everyone turned. The purple-coated man eyed me suspiciously. "Who are you?"

"A troublemaker, Mr. Haskins, that's who," said Bonner. His face turned as red as his bloodshot eyes. "Remove her at once. This is no place for a child."

"If you will allow me a moment, I can explain," I said, stepping forward.

"Mr. Holmes!" said the official, Mr. Haskins, as he spotted my uncle. "Do you know this young lady?"

"Indeed, she's my niece," he said. "Please, I beg you: let her proceed."

"Very well," said Mr. Haskins. Bonner grumbled. I walked over and rubbed the mark on Midnight Star's forehead, then offered my hand to Mr. Haskins.

"Do you recognize the odor?" I asked, holding it up to his nose. Haskins thought for a moment, then replied, "Bleach?"

"Precisely," I said. "I first noticed the smell before the race. It reminded me of a laundry." I pointed a finger at Bonner. "I propose that he made that star by applying bleach to Incredible Start's forehead."

"Incredible Start?" said Mr. Haskins, raising a bushy eyebrow, "but the horse here is Midnight Star."

"He's Incredible Start with a bleached star on his forehead," I explained. "His exact twin was the horse Sir William raced."

"Do you mean to say that Midnight Star is really Incredible Start?" said Sir William. "This is terribly confusing."

Bonner sneered and shouted, "This is preposterous! How could I have found such a rare horse?"

"No doubt you discovered the twin while cheating the city carriage drivers last year," I said calmly. "The horse Sir William raced today has worn shoes. It is not a race horse—it's a workhorse used to pounding our cobbled streets."

"Outrageous!" thundered Mr. Bonner. He reached for the money in Mr. Haskins's hand, but the official quickly yanked it away. "Not so fast," he said. "First, I think we better take a good look at Sir William's horse."

"I won fair and square," Bonner grumbled.

"If so, then you have nothing to fear," said my uncle. "However, if my niece is correct, then you'll be facing charges for stealing Incredible Start."

Bonner looked around desperately. "I don't have to put up with this," he said. He took two steps and vaulted onto Incredible Start's back. "Gee-up!" he yelled.

For a moment everyone froze—everyone but me. I grabbed Bonner's leg as Incredible Start ran by. "Eeee-yow!" yelled Bonner, tumbling from the horse. Ker-flop! He landed on his back, sending up a cloud of dust. "Ooof!" he grunted.

"Incredible Start's original owners can confirm my suspicions," I said, dusting off my hands as Mr. Bonner moaned on the ground. "Incredible Start's name doesn't describe the way he races, but the way he started in life: as a twin."

"A twin?" said Sir William. "That makes perfect sense."

"Why, that's it!" exclaimed Uncle Sherlock. He put his hands on his cheeks and chomped on his pipe so hard I thought he might bite it in two.

"What is it, Holmes?" asked Sir William. My uncle shook his head in amazement.

"Shannon just solved the Baron's Bank case!"

"I did?" I said.

"Indeed, I think you did," said my uncle. "I'll wager that one of the bank's employees has an identical twin."

"Of course! It's entirely logical. One twin could have walked off with the money while the other was elsewhere in the bank establishing a perfect alibi," I said.

"The situation was so elementary, I couldn't see it staring me in the face," said my uncle. He clapped me on the back. "Shannon, you're a genius."

I beamed at my uncle. I couldn't believe it. I'd solved my first crime, and then my second, and all within a minute!

"Miss Holmes, you appear to have a great detective career ahead," said Mr. Haskins. He turned to Henry Bonner. "And you, sir, are about to begin a career as a prisoner." Bonner just snarled at me.

My uncle took off his cap and placed it on my head. "You're a master sleuth, Shannon, if I've ever seen one."

Master sleuth! Though the cap was three sizes too big, I thought the title was a perfect fit.

Ang Pemba and the King's Riddle

AN ORIGINAL STORY BY TIMOTHY TOCHER

Nepali Words:

Sherpas (pronounced "SHUR-pa"): guides and porters in Nepal who lead groups of climbers into the Himalaya Mountains.

Gurkha (pronounced "GUR-ka"): an ethnic group in Nepal who are famed as fierce soldiers.

Ang Pemba bound her hair in the tightest bun she could form and forced it under a woolen cap. There were no mirrors in her hut, but she knew that in her brother's pants and baggy shirt, she looked like a boy. She was ready to try for a position as a royal *sherpa*.

Ang Pemba's people lived on the rooftop of the world—the Himalaya Mountains. She greeted each dawn by staring at the icy face of Mt. Everest, which loomed over her village. In summer, foreign climbers arrived to attempt to scale its heights. Her dream was to go along on these expeditions. Several young men from her village had done just that, but never a girl.

Now the king of Nepal was picking young people to be added to his official crew of *sherpas*. The king's representative would be in the next valley this very day to test the applicants. Those who were selected would be trained to carry oxygen and supplies up the highest mountain in the world.

By the time the sun had fully risen, Ang Pemba reached the next valley. Near a stream, eleven boys from surrounding villages chatted nervously to each other while they waited for the king's delegation to arrive.

Finally, a Gurkha soldier walked through the pass. He was followed by more Gurkhas, each one leading a mule. Behind them, riding on a stallion, was the king's representative. His uniform was covered with medals and ribbons while those of the other soldiers were bare.

While the mules drank at the spring, the Gurkhas unloaded twelve cone-shaped blanket packs from their backs. Then the king's representative dismounted and addressed the group.

"I am Major Nima, sent by His Majesty to see if any from this area are fit to serve as royal *sherpas*. One more person is needed to fill our next class. These packs," he said, pointing to the blankets, "weigh forty pounds. You will each carry one and follow me up the trail. Those who can not keep up are not fit to be royal *sherpas*."

Major Nima handed the reins of his horse to one of the Gurkhas, then turned and walked off, followed by the other Gurkhas and their mules. Ang Pemba smiled to herself. She had been carrying sacks of potatoes over these mountain trails her whole life. She squatted in front of her pack and pulled its straps across her back. Then she stood and walked up the trail.

By noon the group of hopefuls had been cut in half as boys dropped their packs or fell behind. A Gurkha in the rear collected the abandoned packs, which he loaded on a mule. The failed candidates were sent home.

Ang Pemba rounded a curve. The trail dead-ended in one of the sheer drops that make Himalayan treks so dangerous, even in summer. A chain-link bridge stretched across the chasm to a neighboring peak.

Major Nima sat at the foot of the bridge and waited.

He ordered everyone to drop their packs and drink some water while he explained the next test.

"In addition to strength and endurance," he said, "a *sherpa* must also be sure-footed and fearless. Each candidate must cross this bridge wearing a full pack and carrying an oxygen tank. Those who stumble or drop part of their load will be eliminated."

Ang Pemba saw that the floor of the bridge was made of chain links—each only six inches wide. Two handholds supported the bridge while thin wires connected the chain-link steps to the handholds. Between the steps, there was nothing but air.

Major Nima crept across, gripping the handholds while the bridge swung sickeningly in the wind. All but one of the Gurkhas followed. The last Gurkha stayed with the mules.

One of the boys turned and started back down the trail, having decided he didn't want to be a royal *sherpa* after all. Five candidates remained.

Ang Pemba smiled. She had crossed such bridges many times in her life. She knew how wildly they could swing, but she was as expert at riding their motion as a sailor on a pitching ship at sea.

As she waited her turn, the first boy walked out

onto the bridge. He had one terrifying moment when a sudden gust rocked the bridge. But he spread his legs, held fast with his free hand, and kept his balance.

A second boy crossed safely and then it was Ang Pemba's turn. She walked across as calmly as if she were on solid land. The Gurkhas made small sounds of approval until Major Nima silenced them with a glare.

As Ang Pemba watched, the next boy stepped onto the bridge. From his first step, she knew that he was in trouble. His body leaned toward the heavy tank and the way he tugged at the handholds added to the bridge's motion. In midspan, the tank banged against his leg and slipped free. The boy tried to catch it and fell.

The spectators leapt up as one, then sighed in relief. The boy had caught the bottom of the bridge with both hands. But how to help him?

Ang Pemba crawled rapidly toward the frightened boy. When she reached him, she lay flat on the bridge, pulled out her knife, and cut free the straps of the boy's heavy pack. Then she put away her knife and reached down and grabbed the boy's arms.

One of the Gurkhas came up behind Ang Pemba and grabbed her feet with his strong hands. Then, as Ang Pemba held onto the boy, the Gurkha pulled her backwards. Soon the boy was back on the bridge.

Once back on solid ground, the grateful boy embraced Ang Pemba. As she pulled away, her woolen cap popped off, revealing her mound of hair.

"A girl!" yelled one of the Gurkhas. "No wonder he slipped. Women are a jinx on an expedition!"

The Gurkhas brandished their rifles to chase her back across the bridge. But Ang Pemba refused to be bullied. She turned and looked Major Nima in the eye.

"Where were these brave soldiers when the boy slipped? By the time they decided what to do he might have fallen to his death. I have passed each test and deserve to stay," she insisted.

Major Nima was amused by her daring. "My orders say to test all who come, though I am sure no one expected a girl to try. The hardest tests remain. You have earned the right to compete."

The Gurkhas lowered their rifles and sat. Everyone turned to watch the last youth attempt to cross the swinging bridge, but he was gone. Seeing the previous boy almost fall had convinced him that he did not want to take the risk.

"Excellent!" said Major Nima. "Three candidates remain. All have proven their courage, stamina, balance, and strength. Now we will test these qualities at high altitude."

He and the Gurkhas began leading the group still higher. They climbed the steepening trail until Ang Pemba's wiry muscles ached from the cumbersome tank and the heavy pack. Then one of the two remaining boys dropped his tank and quit. The Major gave him some money and food before sending him back down the trail. Ang Pemba and one boy remained.

They climbed for another two hours until patches of snow dotted the shady spots on the trail. Ang Pemba could tell that there was less oxygen in the air, for her lungs burned in her chest. Only her determination to succeed kept her moving.

At last Major Nima called a halt. The group gathered under an overhang and ate a meal. Ang Pemba's fatigue and hunger were so great that the simple bowl of cold potatoes and water tasted like a feast. After the meal, Ang Pemba expected the climb to resume. But Major Nima said that the final test would be conducted here.

"You have proven that you are up to the strain of being a royal *sherpa*," he said. "Now we will see if you can think clearly at a high altitude. I will pose a riddle that the king told me. The first person to solve it wins.

"A *sherpa* is bringing a leopard cub, a chicken, and some grain to the royal court as tribute. He reaches a gorge with a single bridge. The bridge is so narrow that the *sherpa* can carry only one of the three items across at a time. If the chicken and leopard are left together, the leopard will eat the chicken. If the chicken and the grain are left together, the chicken will eat the grain. How can the *sherpa* deliver all three items without carrying more than one at a time across the gorge?"

Ang Pemba and her rival stared at each other. The boy closed his eyes. Ang Pemba tried to clear her mind. "Think of the riddle and not what is at stake," she thought.

Ang Pemba knew she would take the chicken across first. It was safe to leave the leopard and the grain together. But then she was stuck. If she took the leopard next, it would eat the chicken while she crossed back to get the grain. If she took the grain, the chicken would eat it when she returned for the leopard.

Ang Pemba thought until her head ached from effort and lack of oxygen. She peeked at her opponent from time to time and thought that he looked as confused as she was. But then the boy spoke.

"I have the solution, Sir," he called out.

Ang Pemba's heart nearly stopped as Major Nima signaled the boy to speak.

"Since there is no way to avoid leaving one of the animals with its food, I would not try. I would feed the grain to the chicken, then allow the leopard his feast. Then I would deliver the leopard to the king with the chicken and the grain inside it."

Major Nima frowned. "Let us hope His Majesty never puts you in charge of the treasury. Your solution loses two of the three gifts."

Ang Pemba sighed in relief and willed herself to think harder. She pictured crossing the gorge carrying one of the items, then crossing back empty handed.

Then the solution struck her. "I have it!" she yelled. The Major waved his arm for her to proceed.

"First I would cross the gorge carrying the chicken. The leopard would have no interest in the grain. Next I would cross back and get the leopard."

"Ha!" the boy called. "The leopard will eat the chicken. I told you there is no solution."

Ang Pemba turned to the boy. "The leopard won't eat the chicken, for I will carry the chicken back with me and leave it on the original side. Then I will bring the grain and leave it with the leopard. On my final trip I will bring the chicken."

Major Nima and the Gurkhas cheered Ang Pemba's answer. Even the disappointed boy praised her.

"Today I learned that a girl can do anything a boy can do, and even be smarter," he said.

The Major gave him a reward of sixty-five rupees, a *sherpa's* daily pay, and congratulated him on his effort. Then he turned to Ang Pemba.

"I, too, have learned a lesson today. The king never gave me the solution to the riddle, but assured me that I would recognize the right answer when I heard it. You have proven him right."

"Does this mean I get to be a royal *sherpa* and climb Mt. Everest?" Ang Pemba asked.

"It means you will come to Katmandu with me, if your family allows it. There you will go to school. You will learn English, as well as how to climb. If you work hard, you will someday climb the mountain," answered Major Nima.

Ang Pemba gazed at Mt. Everest looming in the distance. After staring from her village to the peak each morning of her life, she knew one day she would stare down from above.

AUTHOR BIOGRAPHIES

Kelli Marlow Allison considers herself a Californian, although she now lives in North Carolina. While in California, she worked as an aerospace technical writer and was very active in several writers' groups, especially the Cupertino Writers. She currently runs her own desktop publishing business and writes in several genres. Her story, "Samantha's Dog-Gone Adventure," is original.

Carol Farley has written many books and stories for young people. Her latest books are *Mr. Pak Buys a Story* and *Korea, Land of the Morning Calm.* Her stories have recently appeared in *Cricket, Challenge, Spider, Pockets,* and *LA Times.* Her online mystery tales can be found at TheCase.com. She is a member of the Mystery Writers of America, The Authors' Guild, The Society of Children's Book Writers and Illustrators, and The Washington D.C. Children's Book Guild. Her story, "Dead Wrong," is original.

Stephen Mooser has written more than fifty books for children, ranging from picture books, such as *The Ghost with the Halloween Hiccups,* to nonfiction, such as *Into the Unknown: Nine Astounding Stories,* to novels, such as *Elvis Is Back and He's in the Sixth Grade!* In addition, he also wrote the first novel in the *Girls to the Rescue* series: *Young Marian's Adventures in Sherwood Forest.* Stephen is currently president of the Society of Children's Book Writers and Illustrators, has two children, Chelsea and Bryn, and lives in Los Angeles, California. His story, "Shannon Holmes's First Case," is original.

Carol Ottolenghi-Barga, author of the original story "Message in the Music," was born in Pennsylvania and has lived for many years in Ohio. Carol is an award-winning writer for children and adults and she stresses adventure, fun, history, and science in her stories.

Jon Picciuolo is a retired intelligence officer who lives near Lompoc, California, with his wife, Pam, and their cat, Dinah. He enjoys hiking and yoga. His stories and articles have been published in numerous magazines nationwide. His story, "Ginger Murphy Goes to Sea," is original.

Patricia Russo lives in New Jersey. She has published stories in *Girls to the Rescue, Book #5, Marion Zimmer Bradley's Fantasy Magazine,* and *Women of Darkness.* Although her original story, "Carmelina," is fictional, it is based on an incident that actually happened to her mother in Italy during World War II.

Diane Sawyer, author of the original story "Chita's Garden," has published stories in many newspapers, magazines, and journals, including *St. Petersburg Times, Writers' International Forum, Short Stuff,* and *Arts and Letters.* She belongs to the Writers' Round Table. She is a docent at the Florida International Museum and the Salvador Dali Museum in St. Petersburg, Florida. When not participating in tennis, swimming, and other fitness activities, Diane enjoys spending time with her husband, Robert, and their children.

Timothy Tocher, the author of the original stories "Lily and the Darters" and "Ang Pemba and the King's Riddle," teaches at George Grant Mason Elementary in Tuxedo, New York. He lives with his wife, Judy, in nearby Rockland County. His humorous poems have been published in *Kids Pick the Funniest Poems* and *No More Homework! No More Tests!.* He has also published five stories in the first two books of the *Newfangled Fairy Tales* series. Another of his stories will appear this year in *Cricket.*

Girls to the Rescue series

Edited by Bruce Lansky

Each anthology in this critically acclaimed series contains folk- and fairy tales featuring clever, courageous, and determined girls from around the world. When girls see this collection, they will say, "Finally! We get to be the heroes." This groundbreaking series updates traditional fairy tales for girls 7–13.

Book #1   Order # 2215
Book #2   Order # 2216
Book #3   Order # 2219
Book #4   Order # 2221
Book #5   Order # 2222
$3.95 each

Young Marian's Adventures in Sherwood Forest

by Stephen Mooser

In the tradition of *Girls to the Rescue,* this novel-length story tells the exciting tale of 13-year-old Maid Marian, who must battle wolves and the evil Sheriff of Nottingham to save her father from the hangman's noose.

Order # 2218   **$4.50**

Order Form

Qty.	Title	Author	Order No.	Unit Cost (U.S. $)	Total
	Bad Case of the Giggles	Lansky, B.	2411	$16.00	
	Free Stuff for Kids	Free Stuff Editors	2190	$5.00	
	Girls to the Rescue, Book #1	Lansky, B.	2215	$3.95	
	Girls to the Rescue, Book #2	Lansky, B.	2216	$3.95	
	Girls to the Rescue, Book #3	Lansky, B.	2219	$3.95	
	Girls to the Rescue, Book #4	Lansky, B.	2221	$3.95	
	Girls to the Rescue, Book #5	Lansky, B.	2222	$3.95	
	Girls to the Rescue, Book #6	Lansky, B.	2223	$3.95	
	Happy Birthday to Me!	Lansky, B.	2416	$8.95	
	Kids Are Cookin'	Brown, K.	2440	$8.00	
	Kids Pick-A-Party Book	Warner, P.	6090	$9.00	
	Kids Pick the Funniest Poems	Lansky, B.	2410	$16.00	
	Kids' Holiday Fun	Warner, P.	6000	$12.00	
	Kids' Party Cookbook	Warner, P.	2435	$12.00	
	Kids' Party Games and Activities	Warner, P.	6095	$12.00	
	Miles of Smiles	Lansky, B.	2412	$16.00	
	Newfangled Fairy Tales, Book #1	Lansky, B.	2500	$3.95	
	Newfangled Fairy Tales, Book #2	Lansky, B.	2501	$3.95	
	No More Homework! No More Tests!	Lansky, B.	2414	$8.00	
	Poetry Party	Lansky, B.	2430	$12.00	
	Young Marian's Adventures	Mooser, S.	2218	$4.50	
				Subtotal	
			Shipping and Handling, see below		
			MN residents add 6.5% sales tax		
				Total	

YES, please send me the books indicated above. Add $2.00 shipping and handling for the first book with a retail price up to $9.99, or $3.00 for the first book with a retail price over $9.99. Add $1.00 shipping and handling for each additional book. All orders must be prepaid. Most orders are shipped within two days by U.S. Mail (7–9 delivery days). Rush shipping is available for an extra charge. Overseas postage will be billed. **Quantity discounts available upon request.**

Send book(s) to:

Name _____

Address _____

City _____ State _____ Zip _____

Telephone (____) _____

Payment via:

☐ Check or money order payable to Meadowbrook (No cash or COD's please)

☐ Visa (for orders over $10.00 only)   ☐ MasterCard (for orders over $10.00 only)

Account # _____

Signature _____ Exp. Date _____

You can also phone or fax us with a credit card order.

A _FREE_ Meadowbrook catalog is available upon request.

Mail to: Meadowbrook Press, 5451 Smetana Drive, Minnetonka, MN 55343

Phone (612) 930-1100   Toll-Free 1-800-338-2232   Fax (612) 930-1940